Jedediah Smith

Jedediah Smith

The Story of a Wayfaring Heart

Win Blevins

Copyright © 2020 by Win and Meredith Blevins

Table of Contents

Chapter One 1
Chapter Two 8
Chapter Three 25
Chapter Four 31
Chapter Five 39
Chapter Six 49
Chapter Seven 60
Chapter Eight 68
Chapter Nine 74
Chapter Ten 78
Chapter Eleven 80
Chapter Twelve 86
Chapter Thirteen 92
Chapter Fourteen 102
Chapter Fifteen 107
Chapter Sixteen 114
Chapter Seventeen 118
Chapter Eighteen 122
Chapter Nineteen 128
Chapter Twenty 134
Chapter Twenty-One 143
Chapter Twenty-Two 150
Fitz 159

Chapter One

I feel a hand shake my shoulder and immediately jump up. Here, almost to the Rocky Mountains, a hand waking you can be scary.

But Major Henry waves a thumb at the fire, meaning we should move over there, away from the other men of the brigade, who are still sleeping.

He reaches for the gray, speckled coffee pot and pours black, steaming brew for each of us. I take a cup from him and breathe the aroma deep inside. Whatever his reason for waking me up, I'm grateful for the coffee.

He drinks and then looks at me over his own cup. "Will you take the job?"

I've been waiting for him to ask. He's talked about it, angled toward it, circled it, and slept on it. Finally he's ready.

He says, "Will you take the express to Ashley?"

I know what he means. He wants a man to volunteer to travel alone through hostile Indian country beyond the Arikara villages, nearly two hundred miles away, and to give a message to General William Ashley: Bring us horses, lots of horses.

I've waited while he spent a day and a half working this out in his mind and wondering—Will Smith take word downriver to Ashley, or will the young fellow be wise and say no?

In this case, I know that *no* is the smart answer.

But it isn't my answer. I want to go. Alone.

Henry's partner in this king-sized fur enterprise, Ashley, needs to hear—getting more horses is essential for us.

But Henry likes to ponder a decision, turn it over and over in his mind, like sucking on a penny.

I wouldn't want to be under fire in a tight situation under the command of Major Henry.

Right now the Major is waiting. I look at him and say, "Yes, sure, I'll go."

Henry lets out the big breath he's holding. "I'm figuring two weeks of travel," he says. "By then the general should be close to the Arikara villages. You can slip by them—good idea to do that at night. You should come on the keelboats pretty quick after that."

I nod to show him I understand. Which I do.

"I don't know how many horses the general can handle on two keelboats. We could use a hundred."

I say, "We can for sure." I've been with Major Henry for nearly a year, trapping the waters above this post at the mouth of the Yellowstone River. I understand the situation.

A trapper's job is to work his way up the big rivers and small creeks and set traps where there's beaver sign. Then we come back to check each trap for our catch of the wily creatures, haul them to the bank, and skin them out. These hides are valuable, six dollars a pound in St. Louis. Hats made from the felt of beavers are all the fashion in New York and London, so they say.

Our word for these valuable hides is *plews*. We get it from the French-Canadian trappers who've trapped the waters of the West for years before we got here. Those Frenchies know beaver.

This is how it works: When a trapper has a full load, he packs the plews back to camp on his horse. That means he walks and the horse carries the furs instead of carrying him. And walking back to camp while leading a horse, that's a lot slower than riding back to camp. Every one of us could use a pack horse, maybe even two.

Obstacle: Here in the mountains a horse costs three times as much as it would back in the settlements, and maybe twice what it would cost at the Arikara villages.

That means some one of us has to get word to Ashley before he gets past the villages. Yes, it's a dangerous assignment, canoeing down the Missouri River two hundred miles through hostile Indian country. More dangerous for a man alone than for a group of men. The thought makes my scalp tingle.

So why will I go? I like being alone in this big country. I was glad to come upriver on a boat with a lot of other men, but I would have been happier to come by myself. I want to feel like an explorer. I want to be an explorer. Maybe I like that tingle in my scalp.

Right now I have preparations to make, mainly taking enough to eat. How much? Jerky for the first meal every day. I'll skip lunch. Then supper—pemmican for sure. We've traded for lots of it. So fourteen days' worth of jerky and pemmican.

Jerky is one of the gifts of the buffalo. After we shoot a buffalo, we cut the lean meat into strips, like king-sized slices of bacon. Then we spread the slices out on a scaffold as high as a man's head and let them dry thoroughly in the sun and air. Dried that way, jerky will last for months.

Pemmican is the next step for jerked meat, if you want to take this step. You spread the dried slices out on a buffalo robe and pound the meat to shreds with a rock. Then you mix the shreds with fat, and with berries if you can find any. Last you wrap the result tight in a deer hide, making a big sausage. That way it will also last for months. Most of us mountain men like to eat it sliced and fried.

Howsomever—that's an expression of my father's—howsomever, on this trip I will chow down my pemmican without cooking it. No fires for me for the next two weeks, even low fires that make very little smoke. I don't want arrows sailing into my camp.

Enough for now. I'm going to pack my food and slip away before everyone is awake.

It's an uneventful trip, no troubles, no skirmishes. I thank God for my good fortune.

Once I can see the keelboats, I start thinking about General William Henry Ashley. He likes to be addressed as "General." He doesn't hold that rank in the United States Army, but only in the Missouri Militia. Still, he likes seeing his name printed that way in the newspapers, and as lieutenant governor of Missouri, he gets his name in the papers a lot. When he runs for governor next year and wins, he'll get to read his name even more. He's confident of winning that election, or so he says.

Now I can see the general himself sitting on top of the cabin of one of his two keelboats. He has a cup in one hand, and since it's morning, that's probably coffee.

I take a deep breath, wishing I could taste the coffee. Since my Methodist mother doesn't approve of it, our family didn't drink it. Now that I've come to the mountains, I'm addicted to it. Everything else about me is still Methodist. Despite the influence of the ruffians and ragamuffins I'm around every day, I don't even cuss.

Angling my canoe in that direction, I get a better view of Ashley, and I can see that he's in full uniform, even wearing the doodads that say he's a bigadier general. He sure likes declaring his rank. And I know that he likes the prospect of being the man who expands the American fur trade. After all, others have tried and failed.

When I bring the canoe alongside the keelboat, several Frenchies hurry to help out. Two of them give me a hand onto the boat. Two more haul my dugout canoe out of the current and slide it onto the deck.

Ashley sees the commotion and strides over quickly. As he gets close, he extends a hand and says, "Young Smith, it's good to see you."

I resist the impulse to salute, shake his hand, and get my message delivered right away. "Sir, Major Henry says that for our business to succeed, we need horses, lots more horses."

Fortunately, the general is generous with his coffee. I join him on his cabin, sitting on the wood cross-legged, the way mountain men do. The coffee is hot, strong, and smells even better than it tastes.

After delivering my message, I fill in the details of why trappers need one horse to ride and another to haul the peltries. He understands quickly and agrees. "Now let me think," he says.

While he thinks, I turn my face into the upriver wind and enjoy. We're surrounded by hundreds of miles of plains here, but a river is rich with odors the plains don't have. Rivers are moist and ripe with smells, plains dry and dusty.

After a while he asks, "Upriver where Henry is, at the Yellowstone post, the Indians want too much for a horse?"

"Probably average a hundred dollars a head, Sir."

"I traded with the Arikaras last year, and they'll take less."

"That's good, Sir." I notice that the general doesn't know we mountain men have shortened "Arikaras" to "Rees."

"This may be my last chance to get horses."

"Yessir."

"All right, all right, we'll do it."

Ashley stands up and looks around at the rolling, featureless plains. Then he muses, "What a country. Why does anyone live here? Oh, yes, I know there's game in the timber along the river banks. There are also buffalo, buffalo, and more buffalo on the plains, hundreds of thousands of them. But the plains have no beauty, nothing like the mountains further on."

Now the general pauses to light his pipe. "And the way they live," he goes on. "Get enough to eat, stay warm, nothing more elevated. Well, they do take care of their children. But they haven't invented the wheel, they don't have carriages, they have no art worthy of the name, they... "

He draws on his pipe for two or three puffs. "I tell you, Smith, acquaintance with the white man will be a great blessing for the Indians. Soon they'll be growing crops. Then they'll start businesses and get jobs. They'll build factories. By God, they'll become white men."

He waits for a while, looking at the horizon, or maybe the future as he sees it. He shakes himself, as though getting rid of something. "I asked Henry," he says, "to teach the Indians to trap beaver, but he says they're not interested. Too bad. I would give a world of foofuraw for beaver plews."

Foofuraw are the pretties that Indian women are keen for, like beads and colored cloths.

I hope Ashley is half the man he thinks himself to be. He believes that wherever he goes, he will show the way with his enterprise and lead to a better future. Of course, he will also get rich.

Chapter Two

I'm surprised to wake up this morning with the two Ree villages smack in my eyes. I slept last night rolled up in my blankets here on the deck, and I didn't feel the motion of the boats sailing upstream. I must have slept very lightly in the two weeks of getting here—nervous about my scalp—and caught up on rest last night.

Bleary, I go to the edge of the boat, reach down, cup water in one hand, and splash it in my eyes.

Now I see the general and walk to him. He's with a big, dark-skinned man I don't know.

"Jedediah Smith," says the general with a broad smile, "this is our interpreter, Edward Rose. He speaks several Indian languages and is adept at the sign language."

Shake of hands. I remember now. He's a mulatto, Negro, Indian, and white, and has a big reputation as a fighter.

"I've heard of you," I tell him. "They call you Five Scalps."

"That was fun," he says.

"Fun" is a word that makes me smile. The story is that, single-handed, he attacked a bunch of Minatarees who were forted up, killed five of them, and drove the rest off.

"Ed," says Ashley, pointing at the villages. "Why would the Rees build palisades around their two villages? Those weren't here last year."

"Wagh!" exclaims Rose, answering in mountain man lingo. "Maybe the Sioux. All the lands behind these villages is Sioux territory, and they'd give their kids to be rid of the Rees."

Ashley nods.

I'm wondering if the palisades were built as a defense against us.

Now Ashley tells Rose, "Let's go over to that sandy beach. Last year I met the chiefs there and got things going with presents."

Rose nods his yes.

Ashley hails a Frenchie and tells him to have a skiff loaded with presents for the Rees and then brought around.

"Rose," the general says, "go with him and keep the presents to a reasonable amount."

Rose follows the Frenchie.

"Smith," he says, "I'd like you to come along and see how this works. You've made a good impression on me, and I want you to learn the business."

"Yessir."

We cross to the sandy beach near the lower of the two villages and don't have to wait long. Three chiefs ride down, dismount, and greet us in a friendly manner. Rose interprets what they say. Ashley says he's glad to see his friend Chief Gray Eyes again, and Gray Eyes introduces the other chiefs by name. No hand-shaking—Indians don't do that.

The chiefs are looking at the presents, not at us.

Ashley says, "We come as friends. We ask to pass your villages in peace, and to hunt for our supper on the other side of the river."

Gray Eyes says nothing but reaches down and fingers a handsome Hudson Bay blanket, white with red stripes.

Quickly, Ashley reaches to the underside of the stack of blankets and pulls out a very fine capote, as they're called—a head-to-toe coat with a hood. And this one has been sewn from a red-and-white-striped Hudson Bay blanket.

Ashley says, "We show our friendship by giving you this coat. It will be warm in the winter."

Gray Eyes stands tall and holds the coat against himself, smiling at the other chiefs, preening.

Now the chiefs move toward the line of presents.

Ashley stands in front of them with a hand up. "Permit me," he says. Then he turns to the array of gifts and says, "I give to you honored chiefs of the Arikara nation"—now he picks up each gift as he speaks and gives it to one of the chiefs—"four pounds of tobacco,"—pause—"four tin cups"—pause—"two strands of blue beads"—pause—"and two yards of cloth, one red, one gold."

He steps back and spreads his arms wide.

Now he asks, "Do you want to trade?"

Gray Eyes says, "I will have to hold a council. Will you wait here?"

Rose answers yes in the chief's language.

It's a long wait. I'm thinking of the game animals that our hunters may have brought to the fires on the other side of the river.

In the dusk Gray Eyes rides back to the sand bar. Through Edward Rose's translation he says, "We'll trade tomorrow."

Tonight a hundred Ashley men—at least there are supposed to be a hundred of us—crowd around two big fires on the far bank of the river. The hunters have shot two antelopes and three deer. These critters are being roasted on spits over two big, open fires. Men go up to the animals, cut off a good piece with a butcher knife, and walk away holding the prize high.

I crowd among them. The Frenchies shoulder me off, and I notice that they're crowding ahead of all of us American trappers. Maybe they're possessive about their places in line because they rowed and poled the keelboats upstream against the current this morning while the rest of us just got a ride.

I get to the front and take a good slice. Whatever meat doesn't get eaten tonight will be put on scaffolds and dried tomorrow. Hot, fresh meat is great, but dried meat is OK too.

Satisfied, I find Ashley and Rose talking. The general has eaten—he's paying every salary here. Guessing that I'm welcome, I sit down and say nothing.

"I want forty horses," Ashley tells Rose, "enough to outfit one brigade to take twenty trappers straight west to the Big Horn River and another twenty to go upriver and help out Henry.

"I hear that the Crow village, they welcome our trappers. That right?"

"You bet," says Rose.

"Our outfit going to the Big Horn—can you guide them to the Crow village where they can spend the winter?"

"You bet."

"You welcome there?"

Rose gives a broad smile. "They think Five Scalps is a hero. They also think I was born a Crow."

"And the Crows know the way over the mountains to the western slope?"

"Say they do."

"My idea is for that brigade to cross the mountains and trap the upper reaches of the big river there. The word is, there's so many beaver on that river, you don't have to trap them—you can kill them on the banks with clubs." He smiles broadly. "What do you think of my idea?"

"This child thinks it's damned smart. Long enough the fur companies been going all the way up the Missouri River and gettin' blocked there. What's worse is, blocked in Blackfeet territory, and then they get torn up by Blackfeet."

"You want to guide the outfit on west into that new country?"

"Naw," says Rose, "I thinks I'll stay with the Crows. Last time I'm living with them I had me two wives. Betcha I kin have the same 'uns again."

Now, as though suddenly, General Ashley takes note of me sitting there. "Smith," he says, "I'm impressed with you. You want to take command of this outfit going to the Crows and then across the mountains?"

I want to jump up, but don't. "Absolutely, Sir."

"If you lead this outfit, I'll give you the title Captain. That suit you?"

I repeat with even more enthusiasm, "Absolutely, Sir."

"Then it's settled," he says.

Now he stands up, and Rose follows him into the darkness.

Thrilled, I get up, find my blankets, and bed down on some good grass.

Ashley doesn't realize what a dream he's helping me fulfill. No, not the title Captain, much more. Lewis and Clark found a way across the Rockies, called the North Pass. But it's a poor route across the mountains. The word is that there's a South Pass, and the Crows know where it is. White people don't know, and their maps don't show it.

Now I can be its discoverer.

No one has seen this, but I have been using one of my notebooks to sketch maps of every bit of the West I've seen. I would love to be the man who puts the South Pass on the map. Actually, I want to be the man who changes the maps of this entire continent, the man who erases the word UNEXPLORED from the Rocky Mountains to the Pacific Ocean.

It's true—I that's what I want.

The next morning Ashley, Rose, and I are getting ready for a day of trading.

Ashley supervises the loading of a skiff with tobacco, blankets, kettles, tin cups, Green River knives, fire steels, and other trade items and looks over these goods with satisfaction. He's told me that last year the Rees traded for goods like these with an eagerness so fierce he could smell it.

"If we need more than this," he says to us as we board the skiff, "we'll signal for another skiff and have it brought."

From the left bank the three of us walk with an escort of Ree men up to the lower of the two villages, which stands about a hundred yards from the water's edge. Other Ashley men trail along, carrying the trade goods. This is Gray Eyes' village, and his people are the ones who have agreed to trade.

The escort leads us to the biggest lodge in the village. Inside wait Gray Eyes and the two chiefs who were with

Jedediah Smith

him yesterday, seated around a center fire that's dead out because of the summer heat. Ashley says sidewise to me and Rose, "I traded with these same men last year."

Gray Eyes welcomes us formally, but with reservations. Speaking slowly, the chief says, "My heart is not good toward white men. Some Frenchmen built a small fort downriver since your last visit. During the winter a Sioux woman ran away from her Ree husband."

I think, *Probably a captive trying to escape.*

Gray Eyes goes on. "She ran to that fort. My men followed her there and got into a fight with the men of the fort. And in this fight"—pause—"one of my sons was killed."

Now I can feel silence swelling up in the lodge.

Then Gray Eyes says again, "My heart is hard toward white men."

I watch Ashley think before he speaks. Then, weighing each word, he says, "I am not one of the French white men. Those French and we Americans, we're different tribes, as different as Arikaras and Sioux." He lets those words hang in the air and then adds, "So I am not accountable for what those Frenchmen did."

He gives that sentence time to sit before he asks, "Are you ready to trade?"

Gray Eyes takes in a big breath, lets it out, and says, "Yes."

Ashley calls for the blankets and other goods to be brought into the lodge. His men stack them behind the general and go back outside to wait.

Gray Eyes and the other chiefs pitch into the trading. A horse for a stack of good blankets. Another horse for two boxes of knives, and another for a dozen kettles.

The trading goes on into the evening. Ashley has to order another load of trade goods to be brought on a skiff. So far, he has nine horses, a long way from forty.

Then, suddenly, Gray Eyes changes. He says he won't trade any more for tobacco, knives, fire steels, or tin cups. Or anything, says the chief, but gunpowder and lead.

Gunpowder and lead? Ammunition for Ree rifles?

I'm relieved that Ashley asks Rose, "Who are they going to shoot?"

Rose answers, "Maybe Sioux, maybe us."

The Ree chiefs are looking at each other with question marks on their faces. Without being asked, Gray Eyes says, "We have to defend ourselves against the Sioux. They want to drive us out."

Ashley watches Rose's face carefully as the interpreter renders Gray Eyes' words into English. Then Rose adds, "It's true, what he says about the Sioux. But who knows what's really on his mind?"

Ashley looks at the three chiefs one by one. I can't read their faces and doubt that he can.

Ashley asks Rose, "They have only fusils, right?"

"Yeah."

Fusils are smoothbore muskets, inaccurate compared to the Hawken rifles we Americans carry, crafted in St. Louis with the best technology. Since the barrels have rifling, our rifles shoot straighter and have a longer range.

The general considers. I know he wants to send twenty horses to Major Henry right now. And he wants twenty here to carry a brigade across the country to the Big Horn River and on across the mountains. My brigade. And he wants all the furs we'll send down to St. Louis next summer.

He's looking at a bonanza here, a fortune. And he has superior firepower.

He turns to Rose. "Do we keep trading?"

"It's your decision," the mulatto says. "But the thought makes my asshole quiver."

The general weighs everything. Then he says, as though to himself, "What do men of daring do? They *dare*."

He says to Rose with a half-smile, "You'll just have to pucker up."

The general says to me, "Smith, step outside and instruct my boatmen to row to the keelboat anchored upstream and bring back boxes of powder and boxes of lead."

I obey orders.

It will be expensive. The Rees want a hundred pounds of lead for one horse and a hundred pounds of gunpowder for another. To these prices Ashley just says no. With a few minutes of wheedling, the price comes down.

When we have twenty horses, the Rees suddenly say they're through trading.

The general leads Rose and me outside, preoccupied. Then he says, "Okay, half the men I'll send with you to the Powder River can walk. Or you can trade for horses with Indians you meet along the way. My plan is still workable."

Now he says to Rose, "Stick your head back in the lodge and tell Gray Eyes to bring the twenty horses down to the river. From there I'll figure things out."

So my future for this autumn and winter depends on a man who wants to think himself great.

I'd rather be on my own. But for the time being I'll stay on the sand bar and watch our horses. "General," I say, "I'll stay here. Send some men to help me stand guard on the horses, will you?"

"Sure. You're in command."

He sends twenty men.

In the small hours of the night Edward Rose comes charging down the slope to the sand bar hollering at us. Some of the men on the boats have been dumb enough to slip into the village during the night in pursuit of female companionship. And now one of them, Aaron Stephens, has been murdered.

"The village is in an uproar," Rose shouts. "I expect an attack soon, probably before dawn."

I don't want to fight Indians—that's not my way—but I'm not gonna sit still and be a target.

Right at dawn a fusillade comes from the village and hell breaks loose here on the sand bar. Horses hit by lead balls scream out their pain. So do men. It's a chaos of blood, outrage, and anger. One of the outraged is me.

I can see what's happening. The Rees are firing their poor fusils at us from the tops of the pickets. Whether they're aiming or just lobbing their balls in doesn't matter. Either way their damn lead is flying all around us.

A horse screams, lifts its forefeet, kicks air, and falls onto its side.

Aa-r-r-gh!

Arthur Black yells "Oh, shit!" He's shaking his trigger hand hard and showering its blood on his legs. The flint mechanism on his rifle is smashed. "Shit-shit-shit-shit-shit," he says, pain wrenching each word.

A youngster who calls himself Junebug clutches his throat, and blood gushes between his fingers. He rolls sideways from a sitting position, bleeds into the sand, and dies without a sound.

Now I'm fighting mad.

Pfsst! A ball nicks my right foot and digs up sand.

Damn! Does every hunk of lead have to bite flesh?

My men are milling about in the open. I shout at them, "Get behind the fallen horses and return fire!"

I know the Ree warriors are protected by the tall pickets, and a face between the pointed tops of logs makes a darn poor target. But at least my men are behind the horses.

Whi-i-i-i-ny! Another horse down. The damn Rees trade us the horses one day and shoot them the next.

Pfsst! Pfsst! More lead balls burrowing into the sand.

I test my bleeding foot and decide it will take my weight without screaming.

I sprint into the shallows of the river and holler to the keelboats for help. "Send skiffs! Send skiffs! Get us out of here!"

Men behind me take up the cry. "Help us! Help us! Goddamn it, get over here." Their words come out as a jumble, tripping over each other, hard to understand.

More lead onto our bar, more *pfsst* and more horses screaming.

"Move your asses," bellow my men. "What the hell do you think rowboats are for?"

I limp out of the river onto the sand bar and throw myself down behind a wounded horse.

On the upstream keelboat Ashley peers at us from the deck and hears our shouts. I see him pointing at us and yelling commands at his Frenchies. I make out the words "Can't you see?" and "What the hell are you doing?"

What the Frenchies are doing is sitting down and staring back at the general, stone-faced. Heavy rifle fire? *Sacre bleu! We're not going!*

Ashley strides over to them and yells in their faces. Among his words I can hear, "Move your asses!"

They turn their backs on him and stare at the far shore.

Now I know why the Frenchies have a reputation for cowardice. I don't want them in any outfit of mine.

Okay, I tell myself, *we'll get help from skiffs or we won't.* I shout at my men, "Get cover! Get behind a downed horse!" I see two of the men dive behind horseflesh. "Shoot back!" I yell at all of them. "Shoot back!"

Now the world is a blitz of confusing sights and sounds. The *pfsst!* of the lead balls, the screams of horses, the cacophony of our rifles right around me and the distant muskets of the Rees, the cries of men getting shot, the spray of sand from lead that misses, the sight of men tumbling to the ground clutching wounds.

I get an idea. The upper end of the sand bar has a breastwork the Rees have built. It offers some protection, and it's a little closer to the village.

"Son of a beech!" yells a man next to me, falling sideways onto the sand and clutching the side of his belly. Blood runs through his fingers.

Limping toward the breastwork, I yell, "Get up here! Get to the breastwork!" I throw myself onto the sand and peer between the limbs, poles, and trunks of this defense. I like this little bit of protection, and I can use a horizontal pole to level my rifle.

In my sights, even at this long distance, I can make out what seems to be a face between the Vs of two pickets.

I fire. I think I see splinters of wood fly. The face drops out of sight. *Not a hit! Probably just drove splinters into his face. Still, one less gun firing at us.*

I pick out faces and shoot as fast as I can reload. I think I probably don't hit any Rees, but maybe I'm teaching them not to show their faces to shoot.

A kid named Jerry runs up, flops down beside me, and reloads. Then he exposes himself—he stands up and raises his rifle to fire.

A lead ball glances off the rifle barrel, knocking it out of his hands.

Jerry's right hand jumps to his head. Blood comes out between his fingers.

Jerry sags to his knees, wipes his hand on his leggings, and starts reloading.

Now I can see that the head wound is a scrape along his scalp.

I can hardly believe it. A lead ball deflected off the barrel of Jerry's Hawken and gouged the skin of his skull, but it didn't penetrate.

Jerry yells, "I'll get you bastards!" He sticks his rifle barrel through an opening in the breastwork and fires.

I think, *I'll take two of this kid,* and fire at a V in the pickets.

For long minutes Jerry and I fire, shoulder to shoulder. Then he turns his head, exclaims something, gets to his knees and then his feet, and dashes down the sand bar.

Two skiffs have arrived.

Terrific. I see that the oarsmen are fellow trappers, not Frenchies.

I limp toward the boats.

The oarsmen are hollering, "Let's go! Let's go! Let's get out of here!" Then they squat down behind the poor protection of the gunwales. But they keep shouting their words of rescue. "Let's go! Let's get out of here!"

Eight or nine of my pinned men dash for the skiffs. One doesn't get there—he cries out, gets tangled in his falling rifle, pitches face down in the sand, skids, and doesn't move.

The skiffs start rocking with the weight of men jumping aboard. The oarsmen heft themselves out of the water and back to their positions.

As the skiffs pull away from the sand bar, one man climbing aboard falls off backwards. Another gets halfway up with a leg on a seat but splashes back into the river. After several attempts to push himself up and get a leg into the boat, a third gives up. All three sink into the brown river, not to be seen again.

The skiffs are rowing back to the keelboats. I didn't make it. Several of us didn't—we're stranded.

One of the skiffs gets back to a keelboat and unloads its passengers.

I see, though, that one of the oarsmen on the other skiff got shot. He's crumpled up on the floor of the boat, clutching his thigh. After a little drifting, one of my men replaces the wounded oarsman, and the boat pulls back against the current and gets to a keelboat.

I can see that about half of our horses are down, wounded or dead. The others have taken to swimming the river. Maybe they can be rounded up later, maybe not.

Now I look back to see a mass of Rees advancing on foot. I want no part of these warriors, and neither do the men stranded here with me. They swim for the keelboats. I see some going strongly and some flailing and sinking.

I take a last couple of shots at the cussed Rees and drop both.

Then I too abandon the sand bar. I stick my rifle in my belt, wade out, and swim for it.

When I get to a keelboat, a husky one of my comrades reaches out and heaves me onto the deck.

I flop down, arms and legs akimbo. I inspect my wounded foot. The ball just clipped the callous of my heel. It will be OK in a few days.

Soon General Ashley comes, squats, and offers me a glass. "Here, Jedediah, this will perk you up."

"What is it?"

"Good whiskey I keep for myself."

I shake my head no. "Thanks anyway." *Ma, I apologize for cussing—just a little bit—but I'm not going to drink booze.*

I ask, "Why in hell were those skiffs so slow to come?"

"The Frenchies let you down," Ashley says. "They just refused to row to the sand bar."

I'll stow that memory as a permanent black mark. You can't rely on Frenchies.

Ashley says, "Would you like a cup of coffee? I just made myself a pot. I can go below and bring it up."

"You bet."

So, after that awful battle, as survivors, we drink coffee side by side, me sprawled out and him squatting.

And I think about this man. He traded the Rees the lead and gunpowder these Indians used to shoot at us.

On the other hand, Edward Rose was part of that trading, and Rose knows about Indians. So the matter isn't clear.

But the result is an outrage. Twenty men were guarding twenty horses on that island. I fear that a dozen of each are dead.

I won't forget it. Lesson: Yes, the first choice is to trade with Indians, always. And when that doesn't work, watch your ass.

Now I apologize in my mind to my mother for cussing, and with my father's good will, I say to myself, "Watch your ass."

On the general's orders the keelboats drift downstream with the current. I'm glad. Our proximity to several hundred Ree warriors was damned uncomfortable. We weigh anchor beside an island and make camp there. I judge that the island is defensible.

Two more men have died on the float downstream, Reed Gibson and John Gardner. Late in the afternoon, before supper, we bury them.

And at their graveside I surprise a lot of my comrades. I've told General Ashley I want to lead this burial ceremony, so I stand beside the open graves with my Bible in one hand. And now I raise my voice to God in heaven, praying:

"Our Father who art in heaven, all present know Thy sternness. Now we ask for Thy help to understand and affirm Thy compassion."

I take a deep breath and go on: "As we now ask for Thy blessing and Thy protection, we ask Thee to receive in Divine love the souls of our comrades Reed Gibson and John Gardner. They died fighting for the right, and now they seek haven in Thy divine arms. Lord, grant them Thy peace.

"Heavenly Father, we stand beside the graves of our comrades in grief. At this difficult moment let us be grateful for the great gift of life. Amen."

I look around at my friends. Maybe they're surprised at the Bible in my hands, the thoughts in my mind, the words I have spoken.

So be it.

Chapter Three

The next morning Ashley calls me in for coffee again, and Edward Rose with us. I draw the smell of the coffee deep. It works against the thunderous expression on his face.

"Two lessons are staring right at me," Ashley says. "One: Indians are treacherous. Count on it."

Rose speaks up: "Rees more than others. I don't know any Crows like that."

The general looks at Rose for a long moment and then nods.

"Two," he goes on, "the Frenchies are worthless under fire. You men I hired in St. Louis, even those recruited from the grog shops and other sinks of degradation—you trappers held steady and fought back. But the Frenchies, these fellows will do the grunt work of getting boats up a river, but when it comes to a fire fight, they wouldn't stick by their mothers. In fact, I have reason to believe that right now they're getting ready to desert us."

Rose says, "Let's go up and put it to them."

Surprise flashes across Ashley's face, but he says, "Why not?"

On the deck he calls all the Frenchies together. "How many of you," he says loudly enough for all to hear, "are willing to stay with me until we can be reinforced by men down from the Yellowstone?"

No answer.

"Stand up, those willing to stay."

Only two dozen stand up. About four dozen more have made up their minds to go back downriver, regardless.

"The rest of you..." He hesitates. "Take the smaller of my keelboats. Float down to Fort Kiowa. You can look for employment there. I'll put the rest of my trade goods on your boat. Leave them at the fort and I'll pick them up on my way downriver."

He draws himself up and gives them a look that means, 'Get out of my sight.'

They make themselves scarce.

Ashley turns to Rose and me. "More coffee?" he says.

We go below and he starts another pot. Until the pot is ready, he sits off to himself, wearing a dark look. Then he pours each of us a cup, stands up, and says, "I will write to Colonel Leavenworth. I'm confident that he will agree with me that the Rees must be taught a lesson. Also, the Missouri must be open to all upriver traffic. So we have to teach them a lesson. I'll ask him to put his forces into action against the Rees, and to ask the Missouri Fur Company to pitch in too."

Now he sits down and gives himself time to sip the coffee. It's hot and good.

Over the rim of his cup he says, "I need a volunteer. Two volunteers. I want to send an express to Major Henry— yes, clear to the fort at the mouth of the Yellowstone— an express asking for reinforcements. We need more men.

"Perhaps more important to the Ashley-Henry enterprise, we need more men for the mission of finding the way across the Rocky Mountains and reaping the bounty of furs on the west side.

"Smith, you brought an express down from the Yellowstone. This time I want to make doubly sure of the safety of the express. So..." He seems to muse. "The trip is two weeks each way. If you two will take the message to Henry, I'll pay each of you a bonus of twenty dollars. That's more than a month's pay."

Rose and I look at each other seriously. Sure, I'm willing to travel with Five Scalps. Who better?

We break into big smiles and shake hands.

"Yes," I say to Ashley enthusiastically.

"Sure enough," says Rose.

It's an easy trip upriver. Ed insists on taking most of the time in the stern, where the hard work is. He's bigger than I am, and either spot is fine with me.

He tells good stories. I wonder how many of them are true. Well, how many are entirely true. When a mountain man tells a story, exaggeration is part of his art.

I like having a friend who's a man of color. Back home in Ohio we didn't know any such folk.

Major Henry is alarmed at the news of our defeat at the Ree villages, and he sees urgency in the situation. He sends word to his trappers up and down the creeks. Within two days more than twenty men are back at the fort, and the next day we're all on his keelboat floating down to Fort Kiowa, where General Ashley is. And there the news is even worse.

I get the story second hand:

Ashley aroused Colonel Leavenworth into action. Leavenworth contacted the Indian agent for the district and Joshua Pilcher, the leader of the forces of the Missouri Fur Company, the rival fur outfit to Ashley-Henry. They all agreed that the honor of American arms and the reputation of the United States government in the West demanded strong action against the Rees.

They enlisted the Sioux, long-time enemies of the Rees, to help out. Then marched against the two villages. Unfortunately, the whole affair turned into a farce.

The various forces proved unable to coordinate. When the Americans expected the Sioux to cooperate by attacking, those warriors were having a good lunch in the Ree cornfields. The Howitzer the army brought fired too far. The shot sailed over the village and only dug into the prairie beyond.

Commanders of different groups of soldiers mistimed their actions, and didn't support each other.

Finally came a possible solution: The forces of the United States and the Rees held a peace conference. At this conference they came to an agreement: The Rees would return all of General Ashley's stolen property, and everything would be square.

The next morning all the Ree people from both villages had disappeared into the vast plains behind their homes, laughing all the way. They had mocked the U. S. Army and gotten away with it.

And the river remained closed to all traffic.

The best that Major Henry, Ed Rose, and I can say for ourselves is that we took no part in this mess.

My mind is not on the past. It's on leading my own brigade west on Ashley's big mission. Now, every day, he calls me "Captain Smith" instead of just "Smith." I'm ready, I'm eager.

In the early darkness, while we trappers are feasting on two buffalo brought down today, the general calls me aside. "I'll be sending twelve men with you and Rose," he says. "If there are certain men you want, let me know.

"I've traded for some horses here, enough for you to pack all your gear to the Powder River, but you and the men will have to walk. When you see the Cheyennes, you may be able to trade for enough horses to get yourself and the men mounted. If not, trade for more horses from the Crows, when you get to them. That's Rose's job, to get you to that Crow village and have a good winter. Rose will stay there, and the rest will be up to you."

Yes, South Pass will be up to me.

"Captain Smith, you're only twenty-four years old. Are you up to all this?"

"Definitely."

"You are new to this rank, and some of your men will be older than you. So you must establish authority by how you conduct yourself, by what you do. It's true that you showed your colors on the sand bar, and the men respect you for that. From now on you must be strong and clear with them every day. No shillyshallying."

He waits, so I say, "Yessir."
"Understood and agreed?"
"Yessir."
"Good luck, and courage be with you," says Ashley. He stands and gives me an emphatic handshake. "You are dismissed, Captain."

I slip away, get out my journal, and write down the names of men who have made a good impression on me, men I want in my brigade:

Jim Clyman, a lank, slow-spoken Virginian. After he ran off from the Rees who were advancing from the village, he made an amazing escape from those who chased him.

Bill Sublette, a gaunt Kentuckian with resolve written all over his face.

Tom Fitzpatrick, a likable Irishman my age, smart and in my opinion possessed of the clear head of a born leader.

Silas Gobel, a man of the kind called half-horse, half-alligator on the river, built like a bull and just as tough.

I stop, unsure of what names to add. Maybe those and Rose will be my core.

I'm ready, I'm eager.

Chapter Four

It's late September before I can form my outfit up to move west. Though I don't know half of these men well, I'm raring to get started.

On the first day we walk across desolate plains and then fall into the valley of the White River, which is truly white, sweet, and according to Rose, liable to cause constipation.

The men drink anyway. They hate being thirsty.

The next morning we cut across a wide bend in the river toward a water hole Rose knows. It turns out to be dry, so dry it's not even worth digging in. Water holes are unpredictable that way.

We push on, even though the river is miles away.

Soon we're strung out for more than a mile, me bringing up the rear to watch for strays. Some men are wandering too far to the right or left, and I wonder if we'll all come together again.

Jim Clyman drifts a little to the right of where he last saw Rose—and by luck finds water. He fires his gun as a signal we all hear and leads his horse straight into the liquid. Led by sound, the other men aim for the water and follow their own pack horses into it. They fire their rifles to help bring the rest of us in, and after getting a couple of big gulps down, they shout as well.

Walking and leading my horse, I come on two men who have collapsed in the sand. I bury each of them up their necks to preserve their body moisture and walk on to Clyman's water. Like the others, I lead my mount straight into the hole and soak up the moisture with my pores.

Then I look around at the men. "I left two of our comrades behind, near death from thirst. I buried them in sand to preserve their body moisture. Now that I've made it to this hole, have drunk, and can fill a couple of kettles with water, I'm going back for them."

The men don't know what to think. At the same time they're impressed with my determination and worried about my welfare.

I don't get back until well after dark. The two men I've rescued are so exhausted they just fall into the water and loll there.

The next morning we come to the river quickly. It's beautiful, clear, and timbered on both sides. When we follow it upstream, we have a stroke of luck—we come on an encampment of Sioux. They welcome us, and I decide we'll rest here for several days. The men have had enough stress for right now. Also, more luck—the Sioux are willing to trade for enough horses to give each of us one to pack and one to ride.

I count our blessings.

On we trek, occasionally taking time to down a buffalo for meat. Buffalo tastes so good it raises the spirits of the whole outfit.

After a few days we hit on what Rose recognizes as the south fork of the Cheyenne River and then wander into one of the strangest places of all creation. According to Rose the Frenchies call it *les mauvaises terreres a traverser*, meaning "bad country to travel through." None of us has ever seen such country, and even to Rose it's just a tall tale. It's all ravines, so that there's not a level inch to walk on anywhere. The soil is thick and gluey, clinging to the feet of man and beast, and when you slip down, it sticks to your rump.

We spend all day slogging across this mess, or maybe just a corner of it. That night everyone seems to eat twice as much fried pemmican as usual, me included. Late in the evening I find Jim Clyman sitting by our fire, scribbling in a journal. I hadn't known he kept one. I keep one too, a record of what I've seen so that I can set my maps straight. I'm hoping for publication someday. I keep mine strictly to myself.

But I make bold with Clyman. "Jim, what are you writing?"

"Trying to describe that country we slipped and slud through all day today, Captain. Ah can't think why God would make such a place, nor let it be made." Jim's speech is all Virginia drawl.

"You wanna see?"

I'm surprised at the offer, but I do want to. Later I copy his account into my own journal. He describes it as soil of a

> Pale whitish coular and remarkably adhesive ... It loded down on our horses' feet in great lumps. It looked a little remarkable that not a foot of level land could be found. The whole of this region is moving to the Missourie River as fast as rain and thawing of Snow can carry it.

Though I can't support Jim's spellings, I do support his description.

From these badlands we rise into the Black Hills. I would like to spend more of my days in the piney cool of this marvelous country, which the Sioux treasure above all other places. They bury their dead here. I myself could spend eternity wandering through this beautiful, mountainous country.

From the Black Hills Ed Rose leads us down into broken canyon territory. Here several of our men fall behind and get stuck in a defile so narrow they can neither turn around nor lie down. They spend a miserable night.

I sit down with Rose that evening. "Ed, we're getting toward the Powder River, right?"

"Right."

"Cheyenne country. Friendly Indians."

"Right. Or Crows, also friendly."

"Then why don't you push on ahead, straight west? Load a pack horse with trade goods and take it along. When you come on Indians, either tribe, stay with them and trade for a few more horses. We'll follow your trail, and when we get there, we'll do some more trading. We'll need the horses early next spring, when we cross the mountains to that new beaver country."

Rose grins big at me. "Thinking big, are you, Cap?"

꩜

Five days after Ed went on ahead, as evening comes on, we're making our way through another darn brushy bottom. A big grizzly comes out of nowhere, seems like, hits our line in the middle, knocks one man down, and runs forward along the line.

From out in front I hear the commotion.

"Bear!" shouts the downed man.

Several other men yell, "Griz!"

Two or three shoot at the bear, with no effect. No one runs after the monster.

I come running toward the hubbub and bust out of some brush almost face to face with the bear.

Griz grabs me by the head with its mouth and the middle with its paws and pitches me to the ground with a hard *thump!*

I yell like hell.

Griz pounces on me.

One rifle after another sounds. My men are coming.

The bear lifts up and roars, but doesn't act hurt. Then it roars again and runs off.

My head bumps the ground after the rest of me.

I can see, blearily, the men crowding around me. Clyman says, "Captain, Captain, what do you want us to do?"

How the devil would I know, Jim?

Jim repeats, "What do you want us to do?"

I say scratchily, "Someone go for water."

"You're bleeding," says Clyman. "All over your head you're bleeding." He sounds desperate.

I'm the one who's desperate.

I make my eyes focus and find his face. I say, "You have needle and threat?"

I correct myself. "Thread?"

"Yes," says Jim. His voice is gentle now.

"Get it out"—I heave for breath— "and sew up my head."

Clyman squeals, like it's him who's desperate. He's fishing his possible sack off his back. Soon I see the scissors flashing in front of my eyes.

He says, "I'm going to cut your hair back so I can see the wounds better."

He does.

He studies my face and head. The expression on his face scares me.

"The griz got your head in its mouth," he says. "There's tears next to the left eye and the right ear. You're slashed to the skull on the top of your head, baring the bone, and your left ear is nearly ripped off."

My stomach wrenches violently, and I hear myself moan.

"Stop squirming," says Clyman. "I'm gonna do some stitching now."

I can feel his fingers pushing one bit of skin sideways, drawing another to cover it, and piercing them with his needle. Over and over and over he does that. As he stitches, I drift into a kind of delirium and imagine that the griz is slowly, in the style of a doctor, cutting my head with its claws.

At last Jim stops. I relax and breathe. The griz is gone. "I've done what I can," he says in a tone that sounds helpless, "except for your ear."

Irish Tom Fitzpatrick takes one of my hands. That feels good. My eyes and his hold each other.

"I can't do anything about the ear," says Jim.

I swing my head from side to side and try to speak, but a croak comes out. Then, one by one, like plunking pennies down to pay for something, I get some words out, "Oh. Try. Stitch. It."

I feel like my throat is stopped up. Then it's free and words come trickling out. "Stitch...it...up...one...way ...or the other."

And I go off somewhere, I don't know where or how. Sleep, I suppose.

The next morning I more or less wake up and am more or less alert.

Irish Tom Fitzpatrick is sitting next to me in the only tent we have.

"How do I look?" I ask.

"Like a scarecrow," says Tom.

He gives me a cup of water. It seems like manna from heaven.

Clyman sticks his head in. "How's my patient?"

"In bits and pieces," I answer.

"The men have found water about a mile ahead," he says. "They've moved down there. Fitz and I are staying with you."

I sit up and my head swirls. Fitz supports me with an arm. "Water," I say, like another man might say, "Girl of my dreams."

I reach a hand up to Clyman and he grasps it.

"Up," I say.

They put arms around my waist and pull me to my feet.

I take a couple of steps outside the tent and, even with arms around me, nearly pitch forward.

I scratch out a few words: "Where's this water?"

"A mile on."

I sit down, then lie down, and close my eyes.

When I wake up, the sun is high overhead.

I stand up without fighting for balance. I say to Fitz, "My horse."

"No," Clyman says.

We have a little back and forth. It ends with, "I am the captain, I want to be next to water, and by the heavens I will ride."

My two friends ride almost shoulder to shoulder with me for the single mile. I feel lucky to keep my balance, or for them to keep it.

At the creek I half fall off my horse into Fitz's arms. He takes my weight and helps me slide my feet to the ground. Fitz is one spunky Irishman.

I stumble a few steps to the creek, fall to my knees, and sprawl to where I can scoop water with one hand.

Fitz gives me a cup instead, and I drink and drink.

Then I bathe my face in water.

I don't want to know what my face looks like.

⁂

It's ten days before I feel much stronger. I have avoided seeing my face, even as a reflection in still water.

I want to move along. Instead of ordering us forward, I assemble the men after supper and say I can ride, and want to ride.

After a little discussion they're with me—we will hit the trail tomorrow.

On the way to our blankets, Clyman says, "Diah, you are *some*."

I say, "Thanks, Jim."

Fitz says, "More than some."

Chapter Five

On the move again, we come to a landmark we've been waiting for, the Powder, and ride into the camp of a big band of Cheyennes. I make them some presents, and they welcome us.

After a few days with the Cheyennes, we move out. I can see the Big Horn Mountains to the west, and I want us to do some trapping. I'm feeling strong now, like I didn't get hurt. Women may be put off by my scarred face, but I don't care. In this outfit the scars get respect.

Right away Ed Rose catches up to us with a group of sixteen Crows, big, strapping fellows full of a spirit of play. These men are glad to trade a few horses to us, and now we have plenty of pack horses. We'll need them for the plews we're going to get in the mountains. But the Crows don't want to slow down to stay with us while we trap. They head out for the Big Horn River and, upstream, the big winter camp of the Crows on the Wind River.

We do well in the Big Horns. I trap with Fitzpatrick, who is as inexperienced at taking beaver as I am. Our catch is smaller than what any other pair of trappers gets, but they josh us only lightly.

I like Fitz. He left home in County Cavan, Ireland, and crossed the Atlantic to look for adventures in the West.

He can just look at my face and see what adventures we're going to have.

He and I are comrades.

⁂

Where the Big Horn for some reason changes its name to the Wind River, right there the travelling gets hard. The main village of Crows has come this way recently, and they either killed the game or drove it off. And the November nights have turned bitter. By the time we find the main village in winter camp, we're half-starved and half-frozen.

Ed Rose is here and enjoying his status. The Crows speak of him as one of themselves. When I ask Ed about this embrace of theirs, he explains how one of the trappers of another outfit told the Crows that Ed had been born a Crow but as a child was stolen by whites. Now, according to this story, he has returned to his own people.

He already has a wife and a home here, with a fine lodge of buffalo hides. Next time we see him he's like to have Crow children and to be a chief.

First thing we trade for buffalo-skin lodges of our own. The tribe had a fine hunt of buffalo just down the river, and plenty of buffalo hides are available. We spend some time learning to put a lodge up and keep warm by its fire. I wonder how many of my men will soon have a one-winter wife. Ed says that's fine with the Crows.

They don't seem to put any stock in chastity. Ed's comment about that is, "Damn, think of a herd of buffalo. Does a bull mount one cow and stop? Hell, no, he sets out to put a calf in every one. And a cow, when she's been topped once, does she quit? Not a bit of that. She makes sure she's got a calf inside there. That's how these plains got full and plus full of buffler."

I don't think the Crows would care to hear about the Ten Commandments.

Even so far from settlements, though, I will remember them.

༄

I can't stand the wait. Ed is basking in his double status—he's the long-lost child come home *and* the hero Five Scalps. And about half of my men are enjoying their status as one-winter husbands.

But I think of only two things: Finding the South Pass and recording its location on the map in my journal. Also getting onto the river the Crows call the Siskadee and the Spanish call Green River. No, I don't be expect that beaver are really walking the banks there, ready to be killed with a club, but that's probably a mountain exaggeration for plenty of beaver and easy to catch.

I want to justify General Ashley's faith in me by sending downriver to St. Louis plenty of beaver plews—plenty times plenty.

I've spent a lot of evenings in lodges with Crow chiefs trying to get a better notion of exactly where the South Pass is. One of the problems is that the Crows can't figure out why we want to be anywhere but right here with them. The way they see things, Crow country is better than anywhere else. The Great Spirit has put it in exactly the right place, and anyone can see that. To the west the people paddle around in canoes and eat fish, which makes them pull bones out of the mouths continually. To the east, on the Missouri River, the water is so muddy that a Crow's dog wouldn't drink it. And so on.

In early February I prove to the Crows that white men are crazy. I tell my men to pack their gear on the horses and ride up the Wind River. I have in mind finding a pass the Crows talk about at the head of this river. I don't know whether that's *the* pass, South Pass, but I want to have a look.

It doesn't work. The snow is too deep in February, as the Crows said it would be. We have to retreat to their camp. I'm dejected, even though we're comfortable here.

Now our evening conferences with the Crow leaders get intense. I persuade Clyman to spread out a buffalo robe and pile up sand to show where the mountains are. Then the chiefs can use their hands to mark where there's a gap to the west.

And I see. If I go up the Wind River to the tributary called the Poh-PAH-juh (Popo Agie the way white people will spell it) and then up that river and over to another one, from there we will see a wide gap in the mountains leading to the other side, beyond the continental divide to the headwaters of that fabled Siskadee River, which drains most of the West to the Pacific Ocean.

I feel my imagination stirring. I have sketches of the Lewis and Clark maps. Everyone knows where the Pacific Ocean is. California borders that ocean from the Mexican line north to the Oregon country, and…

It has turned out that Fitz is as aware of I am of what territory is marked UNEXPLORED on the maps of our continent.

I say, "That's half of our continent."

"No," he says, "that's *most* of the continent."

In Fitz I've found a man like myself, hungry to see everything that is unexplored.

I show Fitz, and only Fitz, my sketches for maps of the part of the West I've seen. I even say to him, "I'm making these maps so I can publish them when I get back to St. Louis. Americans deserve to know how big this continent really is, and what wonders of rivers and mountains it has."

Fitz puts a hand on my shoulder. He says, "You want to be the West's next Lewis and Clark."

I smile to myself and slowly nod *yes*.

❦

In late February, though the Crows say it's still too early, I lead the brigade out again. Now I'm reduced to eleven men. Rose will stay here with his two wives, and one other man prefers marital bliss to the risks of the trail.

We push up the Wind River and the Poh-PAH-juh and then make our way down to the Sweetwater River, which flows back toward the Platte and the Missouri. Here the winds are so violent that they've scoured the country even of buffalo. We spend the nights awake, trying to clutch our blanket coats and buffalo robes tighter and tighter. When the light comes and we try to build a fire of pine logs, the fierce winds blow even the embers away.

These winds keep up at gale force every day and every night. Clowning, Fitzpatrick tries to make up a song called "Devil Winds."

Finally, on their own, Fitz and Jim Clyman wrap up tight and move downstream into a narrow canyon. There they find some respite from the wind.

Jedediah Smith

When Clyman sees a mountain sheep on the cliffs overhead, he throws up his Hawken and fires.

Bump, bump, kerlop, the sheep comes tumbling down and lands right at their feet.

"Hot damn," says Clyman with a big grin.

Fitz says, "Fine of the sheep, don't you think?"

The two dress the critter out and haul it back to camp.

"Meat!" Fitz shouts.

I stand up, hold my blankets tight to my neck, clap Fitz on the shoulder with one hand, and say "Good man!"

Fitz tilts his head toward Clyman and says, "Jim shot it."

"Then it come to Mama," says Clyman.

They tell the story in full and get some laughs. Meanwhile, several men are stirring the embers of what fire we have left from this morning and throwing branches on top. The rest of us cut choice slices off the sheep for broiling. But— "Goddamn it!"—the devil winds say no and even the embers blow away.

We eat the meat raw, without even grunts of disgust. Soon we're wrapped up tight and seeking sleep in our separate little worlds. Maybe I get a little sleep that night, and maybe others do.

Toward morning the winds ease off. After a few minutes I smell broiling meat. "By God," says Fitz, "Fire! Meat!"

Quickly the men are crowded around the fire with pieces of sheep on the ends of sticks stuck in the flames. The smell of cooking meat rises strong and rich.

"Eat up!" cries Clyman, like a boatman calling to the boat behind.

I look at my men wolfing down sheep meat and think what a fine crew they are.

When their bellies are full, in the morning sun and the lulled wind, the men catch up on the sleep they missed last night.

But Fitz is restless. He says to Clyman, "Lone wolf, maybe, but lone sheep, no. There have to be more."

So they go looking. Beyond the spot where they saw that one sheep, they come on a sheltered valley with a grove of aspen and—wow!—plenty of sheep on the hillside above the grove.

Still enjoying the Hawken rifle he has now learned to shoot, Fitz stays and enjoys the hunting.

Clyman comes back to tell what the two have found.

Having dozed most of the day away, we file downstream behind Clyman in the twilight and find Fitz with two big fires, sheep roasting on each of them. The men might bring an end to the lives of quite a few of those sheep, except that now darkness rules.

"Boys, eat up!" I call. "The sheep will be there in the morning."

They gorge themselves.

In morning, after a good night without almost no wind, I see that I'm lucky—the sheep are still on that hillside. I don't have to tell the men what to do.

And we do it straight through the next day, when the sheep decide to go somewhere else.

Now that we're out of sheep, it's time to get going toward a spring hunt. I tell the men to dig a hole to hide our valuables—a cache, we call this hole, after the mountain fashion. Here we deposit lead, powder, and other necessities and cover them up.

I consider: After we've found South Pass, if we find it, I'll split the outfit up, some to the north and some to the south. Or if we get to the Siskadee, some upstream and some downstream. Everyone can reconvene here, and we'll float our plews downstream on this river.

As we head out, I call, "Everyone get your tail here by the first of June, or to the first navigable place downstream."

It's a big country. A man can get lost. Indians can intervene. Anything can happen. So a home base will serve us well.

For now we push up the valley of the Sweetwater. But the winds come back, howling out of the north and west, and ground blizzards make us miserable. The snow cakes on our blanket coats. It gets so thick that I call a halt and we pound on each others' cakes to break them.

Fitz come up to me and beats out a rhythm on my chest, singing so that his voice and fists make a drum and bugle corps. My cakes succumb to the beat of Tom's fists.

"You trying to break me?" I ask with a smile.

"Break your cakes, break your cakes," Tom sings back.

Then I shove Fitz to the ground—whumpf! I sit on his belly, grinning, grab the cakes on his chest, pull them off his coat, break them with my hands, and toss them into the wind.

Soon half the men have dropped their reins and pitch in to break ice cakes off the coats of their comrades. The outfit looks like it's rioting, and everyone is laughing.

The horses look at us in stupefaction, but they don't run off.

On the sixth day up from the cache, Fitzpatrick and Jim Clyman, out in front of the brigade, see a buffalo and shoot it.

After going hungry for four days—we're out of sheep meat—the men don't bother with cooking the flesh. They eat it raw as it comes off the carcass.

"Lemme at that meat!"

"It's *good* raw!"

"Get out of my way!"

"Goddamn wind ain't gonna let us have no fire anyhow!"

"You gonna eat it or talk about it?"

I know better than to try to calm them down. At least full bellies make good sleep.

❧

When we pass the headwaters of the Sweetwater River, the route ahead looks almost like a plain. We walk gradually up, hungry and thirsty, trudging. And for quite a while we walk level, and then... downhill?

I'm thinking, *Maybe this is it.*

I wave Fitz up to ride alongside me.

"Do you see what I see?"

"The land is inclining downward a little bit," says Tom.

"And the gullies are winding down ahead," I say.

We look at each other and say at the same time, "South Pass!"

I raise a hand and let all the men come up close.

"Gentlemen," I say— "well, gentlemen and ruffians, we have found the Southern Pass. We have crossed the continental divide and stand here on the waters of the western slope. All streams here head to the Pacific Ocean."

Jedediah Smith

"Three cheers!" someone hollers.

"Five cheers!" yell others.

Inside I am wildly glad. I tremble a little, and my heart does a dipsy doo.

Fitz says, "You did it."

"We did it."

"Now you can write SOUTH PASS on that map of yours."

"This is an easy pass, gentle on the way up, gentle on the way down. Good for wagons."

"A good route for emigrants," Tom says.

I'm silent for a moment.

"Diah, where there's land, there will be emigrants. One day your countrymen—0ur countrymen—will fill up this land acre by acre."

"I like to think of it as wide, wide open," I say. "Look what's out in front of us. Everything that's marked UNEXPLORED on the maps lies open to us to walk across. We can cross the deserts, drink deep of the rivers, climb the mountains, all the way to the Pacific Ocean."

"Let's go exploring," he answers.

Chapter Six

Gullies led down to creeks, and after a while creeks led to the Siskadee, just as the Crows said.

I've been thinking about my small outfit and the big river ahead of us to trap. Also about my friend Tom Fitzpatrick.

One evening I take him aside and say, "Tom, you're a born leader." He looks at me curiously. "A born leader, and this is your first chance, right now, to be a booshway." The Frenchie word for it is *bourgeois*, but we American trappers have twisted it into "booshway."

I see a flash of light in his eyes. He likes what I'm saying.

"I'm going to take six men downstream to trap the main part of the Siskadee and its tributaries. I want you to take the four others to trap the headwaters." I add, "Whichever four you want."

"Understood, Captain," he says.

"Good luck, Captain," I say back.

The next morning both parties ride out, Fitz and his men upstream, me and mine downstream.

My last words are for everyone: "No matter what happens, be back at the cache on June the first."

However, the mountain country has its own say.

My men and I luck into a heaven of beaver country. We work the creeks flowing in on both sides of the river. We work the main river. We work until the plews are piled so high on our pack horses that the poor beasts stagger.

We trap through April and May. I know the dates because my journal is dated page by page. I see June first hit me in the face. We're maybe two hundred miles south from the cache—we're going to be very late getting back. I tease myself gently—the Captain is missing his own deadline.

When we do get to the cache, it turns out that Fitz also missed the deadline, but only by two weeks instead of four. He and his men have opened the cache. That's a good thing because our powder has gotten wet, and he has spread it on the ground to dry.

Now I get to hear his adventures. "I made camp with a family of Shoshones and used my Irish charm to befriend them."

This was a small joke of his, because we'd found Shoshones consistently friendly anyway. "On the second morning we woke up and they were gone, with all our horses. They left the plews behind.

"So we loaded the plews onto our mounts for riding and walked. We followed their trail to the main Shoshone camp and sure enough, there was the family. I made some presents to the chief, told him what had happened, and the good man returned our horses.

"That's why we have quite a few plews to give you, though the episode of the theft cost us some time of trapping."

We had a lot of plews to show him. Our river had been better trapping than his creeks.

Now a problem: I look at the Sweetwater River and see that it isn't deep enough to float even a bullboat. Fitz and I stand on the bank, look at the water together, and grimace.

"Let's check downstream and see if it gets any deeper," I say.

"Uh," says Tom, "that brings up... Clyman and I did that for about fifteen miles—getting deeper but still too shallow all the way. He said he would keep riding until he found a good spot. I came back to camp. That's been a week and... no sign of Jim."

※

Jim Clyman sewed up my face after the griz tore the devil out of it. Maybe he kept me from bleeding to death. When I was desperate, he healed me. Now I owe him.

I ride downstream alone for Fitz's fifteen miles. After another fifteen or twenty I find where Jim camped. Unfortunately, nearby I find where a war party camped—much too close.

I can read sign. I can figure out what happened here.

Sorrow swells in my chest. Yes, the men who come to the mountains to find adventure often find death. But Jim...

I ride back to camp packing a load of grief.

※

In camp see I immediately that the river is running higher. The snowmelt is swelling it.

I set the men to building bullboats. Since this is their first time at this task, I supervise it carefully. They stick one end of each limb into the ground, bend the limb over until it meets another limb planted opposite six or seven feet away, and tie them together. They repeat this procedure until they have a framework like an upside-down bowl. Then they tie buffalo hides to the limbs, overlapping, flip the bowl over, and—presto!—they have a boat shaped like a cup. They cut a stout pole for something to push off boulders and other troubles. The boat is hard to steer, but by the heavens! it will float.

I load the boat with the fur catch of the spring and fall hunts and call Fitz aside. "I want you to ride this floating bowl downstream to Fort Atkinson on the Missouri River. From there keelboats will deliver the furs to General Ashley. He's eager for them. Take two men with you, whichever ones you want."

Fitz throws a mock salute to his forehead, grins, and sets off to talk to the men. This assignment is an adventure, and he probably wants companions who are up for that. The next morning he poles the bullboat into the current, comrades Branch and Stone perched awkwardly on the furs beside him, and they're off.

※

Summers are quiet times for beaver trappers. The peltries aren't worth taking, so we have nothing much to do but feed ourselves. We like to hunt, and all summer long I bring in at least two buffalo a week. We love to eat, especially if the food is buffalo ribs or buffalo tongue. I also take long hikes up and down the river, dragging myself back to camp

very tired. I take rides that are even longer, learning the surrounding country, and bring my mount back to camp thoroughly worn out. After a couple of weeks I find a little waterfall with a pool at the bottom. I strip off all my clothes and loll in the water. If I had soap, I would bathe. I float, relax, think of home, imagine myself at Sunday dinner…
Until I feel the water creeping up my nostrils.

Back in camp I wait for word from Fitz, gone downriver to Fort Atkinson. The wait is impatient and futile.

My men like card games, especially whist and poker. When they play, I sometimes read the Psalms, my favorite book of the Bible. I particularly like Psalm 126, "They that sew in tears shall reap in joy," which I read aloud. I have often sewn in tears, for instance those I shed at the death of my friend Jim Clyman, who had saved my life.

Reading the Bible gives me conflict about the company I keep. Their language is either uneducated or vulgar, they like to get drunk, they gamble, and they are eager fornicators. Yet every one of them—this is my experience—will prove stalwart in the face of danger and will help a companion in trouble.

In the autumn I lead the men west to hunt along the Snake River, which circles the southern edge of Shoshone country and ends in the far land of the Nez Perce. In the spring we trap the Wind River Mountains. We will have a fine cache of furs to give to the general when the time comes. If it comes. After the catastrophe at the Ree villages, I wonder if he will venture into the West again.

We winter with a small band of nearby Shoshones. Knowing where we're camped, they ride in one day and make sign language with me. I've come to understand a little

Jedediah Smith

of it. We're invited to spend the winter in their camp. Starved for company, we agree, and pave the way with some presents.

When the winter ends and the buffalo hunts begin for the Shoshones, I lead the men back to the cache on the Sweetwater. Good chance Fitz will come here looking for his outfit.

But without word from General Ashley or Fitz, I am stuck in uncertainty.

In June, after our spring hunt and a full year since Fitz, Branch, and Stone set out downriver in that big bowl pretending to be a boat, Jim Clyman himself rides into our camp, in the flesh.

"Halloo!"

"You're a sight for sore eyes, you old coon!"

"Damn! Is you real, Clyman?"

"I'm still above ground."

Clustering around, the men cheer for that.

"Good to see ye, hoss!"

"Glad you got your hair!"

"You done look better with hair on."

"Hooray for mountain doin's!"

I embrace Jim heartily.

Yes, those who sew in tears truly shall reap in joy.

First, his news: General Ashley is calling for a rendezvous of all trappers at a certain point down the Siskadee—he will mark the spot by peeling the barks off the trees along the river. Rendezvous is in just two weeks!

We walk back across South Pass and follow downriver for a couple of days.

Hooray! Shining times! My men and I will be there.

Clyman is in luck, and so am I. One of the men downed a buffler this afternoon, hauled it back to camp, and now it's on a spit above the open fire.

I shave slices of meat off the tongue, my favorite part, and share them with Jim. "Healer," I say—I must be feeling sentimental to use a name like that— "Healer, tell me your story. It must be a helluva story."

Whoops, I sorta cussed. Sorry, Ma.

Clyman has the full attention of our crew now.

The first part of his story is simple. "That war party didn't get me on account of they didn't see me first. Soon's I seen them ride in and start making camp, this child done eased, quietly e-a-sed right on out of there. If they spotted my fire the next morning, this'un be *long* gone."

"But after that good start, my tale gonna get darker 'n' darker.

"I slipped downriver secret-like as I could. But—how far is it from where I started to Fort Atkinson?"

"Up towards five hundred miles," I tell him.

"Five hunnert! Hmpph! Wonder I've still got my hair. Anyhow, afore long I get robbed of my horse. Three Pawnees stopped me on the open plains, coulda taken everything I had, but just stole my horse. I still had my rifle and a few balls I could shoot, and still had my knife to cut what I shot with, so I wasn't starving. Not yet.

"Good ways on—seemed like a long ways—I seen a village in the distance, Pawnees again. While I'm feeding on pemmican for breakfast, a squaw who's along in years, she comes down to the river for water and sees me. Then, soon as she sees this 'un lookin' at her, she runs off." Jim smiles and shakes his head. "And comes back right quick with her man."

Jedediah Smith

"Wagh!" exclaims one of my men.

"He makes signs that I kin come to their teepee and eat with them. I done eat, but I see the invitation as right friendly. And I'm lonesome. Lonesome gets big in the great out yonder.

"Ever thin' seems good to me, I'm resting and doin' palaver with these old folks, but that afternoon the chief calls a council. Nobody tells me the outcome of their talk, but when they're finished, a gang of young braves comes to the teepee and right quick they robs me. My rifle, knife, blankets, lead balls, fire steel, flint—everthing I needs to survive.

"And I knows they're waiting until nightfall to take what I've got left, which is my life. By torture, I'm sure—the evening's entertainment is gonna be me. The robbers don't say nothing 'bout it, but I can hear it in the shadows of their words to each other.

"When the young bucks leave, the squaw talks soft to her man, who's old as she is and then some. Between whatever she says, she looks sideways at me, so I know they're talkin' 'bout the white man.

"The old man goes to the door flap, looks outside and sees half dark. He comes back in and busies himself at making something, I can't see what. Finally he takes a peek at the flap, sees the last bit of half-light outside, and makes motions for me to get on my feet. Now he leads me by the hand to the back of the teepee and shows me with one hand how the flap will fold up. Then he tells me with hand motions that he's gonna go outside and around to the back, and I'm to slip out under the flap.

"He does go outside, and his woman makes me feel better with one of the few hand signs I know—'It's good.' Then she brushes me away, like a mama sends a child off.

"The flap slides up, I scoot out on my back, and the old man and I look into the darkness. He leads casual-like between a few lodges and then into the edge of some trees. He stops and points ahead into darker darkness. I make the sign for "good" to him, nod, turn, and pad away quiet as a shadow.

"Owe my life to them good-hearted old folks, this child does."

I say, "Except you got no way to survive."

One of the men claps his hands a little and says merrily, "Clyman, you sure know how to stretch out a tale until it's way tall."

"You wouldn't think it was a bit tall, had you'un a' lived it. And it ain't over, this story ain't."

He has everyone's attention.

"On down the river I walk. After bout' a week I'm hungry as a big ol' bear after a long of winter … hiberkation," he guesses.

"Hibernation," I put in, smiling.

Clyman gives a big nod. "A long winter of hibernation.

"Finally, this yere child ain't had a bite in about ten years. On the last day I find some bones and pick 'em up, thinking to use them like weapons. Silly idea. Not long past that two badgers come along and damned if this child, staggerin', damned if I doesn't kill them badgers with the bones.

"Gnawin' at 'em, I weave on like a drunk, barely keeping my balance. I slant too far sideways, bump against a tree, and then lean against it. I blear ahead, half out'n my mind, and what does I see? Old Glory!

"I fall down, and breathing hard, get to my hands and knees. Them stars and stripes, they is flying above the fort, blowin' in the wind and like singin' a song, and all the words are few— 'Oh-oh say can you see!'

"I kin see, by God, I kin."

"This yere hoss, he don't know if he done crawled or walked to that fort, Then I hollered—it was more like a croak—until the guard let me in. He walked off and come back with a piece of bread and butter. And I here to swear to everyone—EVERYONE!"—bread and butter is the sweetest, loveliest piece of food on God's good earth!"

Seems like he's run out of story.

I slice some more tongue and pour Jim some coffee in my cup. I pat the boulder I'm sitting on as a sign, Jim sits down, and I hand him food and drink.

As he sips the steaming coffee, I put an arm around his shoulders and say, "You're a helluva man, Jim."

෴

After a few days Fitz, Stone, and Branch come in with a story just as wild as Clyman's. Floating down the Sweetwater when the river was high with snowmelt, they got into a tough spot. The bullboat flipped and dumped all three men, their gear, and the furs into the water.

Fitz tells Clyman he's never imagined anything could be so cold. They managed to scramble to shore without drowning, and then realized they didn't know what happened to their rifles. They never did find them.

While they were shivering on the bank, Fitz announced that they were going back into the freezing river for the furs. The other two men did some royal griping, but in the end, being mountain men, they dived for the furs and came out with most of them.

Fitz said he got so cold "The two halves of my arse, they froze into one icy block. I had to lay bare arse up to the sun and wait for it to melt. Even then I was too plugged up to shite, and had to wait some more.

They cached the fur next to a rock big enough to be a landmark visible for miles. Then they walked a route similar to Clyman's without a way to kill even a rabbit. They got to the fort starved, bedraggled, almost ready to quit.

Clyman says, "They come to the fort in a more pitiable shape than even this'un was."

He adds that Fitz put this cap on the story: "After a lot of good meals, I borrowed some horses and we went back after those furs."

And when he got back to the fort, he wrote a letter to General Ashley saying, "I and my companions are at Fort Atkinson and we brought plenty of plews. We'll wait here for you or your instructions."

I think maybe Fitz's letter is why the general decided to risk the mountains again.

When he finally got up to Fort Atkinson, in early November, he told Fitz right off, "This year is gonna drive me broke or make me rich."

Chapter Seven

I have a really long wait to get this full story from Fitz. I see him off in the bullboat down the Sweetwater in one June and see don't him again until two seasons of trapping and a winter among the Shoshones go by.

He finally arrives in June and with the darnedest news, all of it good:

The general is back in the mountains. Not by the river, though. Instead of using keelboats he's put together a pack train, horses and mules, to come up the Missouri to the Platte River, up the Platte to cross the Rockies to the north of South Pass—not a good route, says Fitz. And now the general has called for a rendezvous of all the trappers in the Rocky Mountains, a hello-and-how-the devil-are-you? for every one of us mountaineers in a couple of weeks.

This get-together will be over on the Siskadee. The general will float down a bit from the headwaters and peel the bark off trees on the bank to mark the spot. He's brought powder, lead, blankets, coffee, and everything a mountain man could want, so we'll re-supply with Ashley. He gets our furs and we get what we need for another year. And Indians will trade for what they want, too. They're invited to the party, and the general will trade them knives, cups, kettles, and trinkets for their buffalo robes.

Hooraw for mountain doings!

❦

As soon as we get to rendezvous, General Ashley nods me into the darkness, away from the big fire, for a quiet sit-down. Turns out he has his own small fire.

He lifts a jug, pours some liquid into a cup, and hands it to me. I smell before I drink and hand it back with, "No thanks."

"You don't drink whiskey?"

I smile. "You forgot."

"Know what mistake I made picking goods for the backs of the horses and mules?"

"No." Feels like I know him too well to attach the "Sir."

"Didn't bring any awerdenty. Isn't that the way you mountain men say it? *Aguardiente*, the Spanish word for brandy. Rotgut compared to the Kentucky whiskey I've got."

"It helps get a man drunk," I say.

"Yes, I'm sorry I didn't bring any."

"You could trade your whiskey."

"I have two jugs. They'd last about an hour, and I'd be thirsty all the way home."

To hear him call St. Louis, or the settlements, home—that feels odd. "Home" didn't mean anywhere back that way to me anymore, not even my own home, with my parents. After only two years of being in the West, I feel at home here in the mountains.

"Well, next year, I'll bring a lot of awerdenty, and I'll over-charge for it." He grins at his own small joke.

"So we'll rendezvous again next year?"

"Good idea, don't you think?"

"Very good."

"I'm taking a direct route to the part of the mountains where the most beaver are, not that long and risky way up the Missouri that ends up far north of the best beaver country. Also not past the damn Rees.

"This way you mountain men get to stay out here in the mountains. Most of you are hell-bent to stay here anyway.

"So every summer I'll ride out here with a train of horses and mules, or send a train. It will get to rendezvous, provide what you trappers need for another year in the mountains, and take your furs back to St. Louis."

Send a train? I think maybe he's making room in his mind for his run for governor of Missouri, and even time for being governor. The general is always looking to get bigger.

Now he grins broadly. "Beaver plews are still bringing six dollars a pound in St. Louis, so I'm bound to make a profit."

I can see the advantages. "Depends on the mountain prices," I suggest.

"I won't charge every bit the market will bear, but, yes, I intend to make money.

He goes on, "Think of the other benefits. I get the benefit of not paying salaries to a hundred men. They get the benefit of freedom. They can trap their favorite creeks, winter where it's warm, follow their own judgment. They're *free* trappers. The man who's the best trapper makes out the best. What do you think?"

"It's good. It will work. And some men," I add, intending a twist of humor, "will get to spend the winters with their Indian wives."

"And even their Indian children," says Ashley. "But we're getting ahead of ourselves. You like this set-up."

"It's very good. In fact, I was thinking of saying to you that a pack train would be better than a keelboat."

"We're on the same track," he says. And now there's a new tone in his voice. "Captain Smith," he says, "you're a good man, very good. You led my party out to the Crows to winter, you found the South Pass, you capitalized on first-rate beaver country right around here—you're a first-rate leader. Your contribution helped me pay the back the money I borrowed to fund last year's enterprise and gave me the capital to buy the goods all these men are trading for."

He gives me a look I don't understand. "Are you interested in business?"

"Of course, Sir."

"All right, here's some news. Major Henry has opted out of the fur trade. He's no longer my partner—he took no part in funding this pack train.

"And that, Captain Smith, opens my mind to a new possibility. This fur business I'm into, it would do well with one partner in St. Louis where the beaver has to be sold, the pack train put together, and the next summer's trade goods purchased—one partner in St. Louis for the business end and one partner in the field for the mountain end of things. Will you consent to be my partner? Ashley-Smith?"

I'm stumped.

"Young man, I'm offering you a fifty percent share of an excellent business without your investing a single dollar. I'm investing in your character."

I manage to fumble out "Yes." That's all I can manage.

"One more bit of business," he says. "You've been my field leader for a year. I want you to go with me to St. Louis at the end of this rendezvous and help me put together a pack train that will start back to the mountains immediately. That means you won't be in the mountains this fall or winter. And *that* means we won't have field leadership for the fall hunts.

"So I want to appoint two captains to step into that vacancy. Will you make suggestions?"

"Yessir, Tom Fitzpatrick and Bill Sublette, both first-rate men."

The general gives an odd smile. "I like Fitzpatrick," he says, "but I think he has a gift for misadventure."

Considering Fitz's troubles getting downriver to Fort Atkinson, I can't disagree.

"So call me superstitious," he goes on. "Can you suggest another man?"

"Sure. David Jackson." Another very go0d fellow, and the only other one in my head.

"Where should they lead hunts this fall?"

"The headwaters of the Siskadee and out west along the Snake River."

Ashley stands up. "All right, said and done. I'll give them their promotions tomorrow morning, and their hunting assignments."

It's all I can do to stand up and shake his hand before he walks away. My head has gone willy-nilly with all this news.

❦

That night, wrapped up in the one blanket I need in the summer, I try not to question myself. The trip to St. Louis and back, that's all right. Making money, that will be good. But I have to wonder: My great big ambition is to see the rest of the West. I want to find the best route across the continent to California—maybe more than one route to California. The best route to walk from California north to Oregon—and back. To see what mountains may rise between here and California, and in the Oregon country. To cross whatever sandy deserts may stand in the way of all this travel. And most of all, to fill in my maps, which will change the published maps of all of this continent between the Rocky Mountains and the Pacific Ocean. To draw sketches of all of those lands in the journal I have reserved for my own maps. And to publish my maps. Yes, publish them.

A while back Fitz said to me, "You want to be the next Lewis and Clark."

Yes. Yes, I do.

I roll and face the other way. For now one duty is enough: I will be a good partner to General Ashley. I will honcho the pack train to St. Louis, help buy next year's supplies, and march the next pack train back.

Enough for now. Enough.

But hours later, still awake, I sit up, get one of my journals, and start a letter home to Ohio:

October 5, 1825

Dear, Mother, Father, brothers, and sisters—

I'm sorry I haven't written you since the spring of 1822, when I first signed on with General William Ashley to go to the Rocky Mountains as an employee of his company, Ashley-Henry. At the time I was one of about two hundred employees of this firm, which is the major force in the American fur trade.

The intervening years have brought many, many adventures, some very dangerous, and some big changes in my life. Here are the changes:

In the summer of 1823, because of my performance in the field, General Ashley promoted me to the rank of captain and assigned me to the command of a brigade intended to reach for the first time beyond the Rocky Mountains in the hunt for beaver pelts. In crossing to this region my men and I sought out and discovered the South Pass, an easy route across the mountains, suitable for wagons and emigrants when Americans move West.

I am making maps of the areas I go into as an explorer, and my great desire is to take the word UNEXPLORED off all of the areas of the West.

This year General Ashley has reorganized his company and, I'm happy to say, has made me a full partner is his firm, which is now Ashley-Smith.

I write to you now because I have about to travel back to St. Louis for the first time in three years. From that city I can send a letter via the United States Mail Service.

I miss my family, sometimes painfully. My company here is uneducated men whose speech is rough and sometimes vile. They are also drunkards and are sexually loose (Mother, you would NOT approve of their language or their behavior). However, when we are in trouble, or even under fire, they make stalwart comrades. That's what counts.

I also miss the fellowship of a Christian church. Sometimes, when I turn the page of my journal and it announces a Sunday, I daydream about myself in the midst of a congregation of like-minded people singing a hymn like "What a Friend We Have in Jesus." And that fantasy merges into a picture where I am eating Sunday dinner—fried chicken and mashed potatoes! —with my beloved family.

    I long for that day, but have no idea when I may be able to make it a reality. My new responsibilities as a partner in Ashley-Smith will prevent me from leaving the mountains for the long trip home until a time I cannot determine.

    In the meantime I am

Your dutiful son and brother,
Jedediah Smith

Chapter Eight

As a firm Ashley-Smith takes in almost nine thousand pounds of beaver at this first rendezvous, paying three dollars a pound in trade goods. The general and I start the pack train back to St. Louis on July 2 and plan to spend three months on the trail. We will get about fifty-five thousand dollars for this beaver in St. Louis. Seems handsome.

After marching throughout July, August, and September, we arrive in St. Louis on October 4. That night, in the general's house, I look in a full-length mirror for the first time since my fight with Sir Griz, and the sight of my face makes me jump.

Though I'm the general's partner, I don't want even his secretary to see me. My face looks like a stretch of sand crisscrossed by red wagon tracks. How can I present myself to the society Ashley probably meets routinely? What response would a beautiful woman have to me except horror? How could I show myself in a church?

After his big fight, Ed Rose got the name Five Scalps. Probably the Crows will call me Fifty Scars.

My duties, though, are spent among men interested in my wallet, not my face. For twenty-five days the general and I keep busy bargaining for horses, mules, saddles, and guns, not to mention the countless items we will trade to my fellow trappers and to Indians, including those the general didn't think of for the last supply trip, like sugar and awerdenty. During this time I'm also busy hiring the men who will lead our horses and mules and, if necessary, fight off Indians trying to rob us of everything.

One day I witness the marriage of General William Ashley to Miss Eliza Christa. At that event I am acutely embarrassed to be showing my face, and all the more embarrassed because the event brings out the finest social display St. Louis can offer. I would feel more at home in council with Crow chiefs—they don't criticize in English.

After just three and a half weeks in St. Louis, on October 29, I'm in command of this big outfit back to the West—seventy men and a hundred and sixty horses and mules. We've spent twenty thousand dollars on the merchandise on the backs of our animals. After a few digits such numbers bewilder me, but I'm clear that the general and I are making a profit.

Those weeks were a whirlwind of business, and I learned something: I definitely want to run the field end of our enterprise, not the city end. I'll take a cold creek, a steep mountain, or even an angry Indian over wrangling with stubborn horse dealers.

Our return to the mountains goes smoothly. We cross South Pass, hit the Siskadee high up, then travel north and west to Cache Valley, which lies to the northeast of the Great Salt Lake. The Valley got its name because some of our men dug a cache there, and we've found it a good, warm place to winter. The general has designated it as the site of our second rendezvous, set for July, 1826.

Jedediah Smith

At the start of that rendezvous I am startled by a new proposition from General Ashley. He asks me, Bill Sublette, and Davey Jackson to stay and talk one night after a good feast on buffalo. In the flickering light 0f the big fire he makes us an offer: Sublette and Jackson, he says, have served the firm of Ashley-Smith very well as brigade leaders. So why should not they join me and together we three will form a new partnership of highly skilled leaders of beaver hunts? Smith, Jackson, and Sublette.

Right away that sounds good to me.

For himself, no, Ashley will not be retiring from the fur trade, just restricting his role to supplying rendezvous. At this moment I am struck by a realization: The general sees that supplying the large of band of trappers out here is reliably profitable. Running the business of trapping beavers, on the other hand, is risky. He is being a businessman first.

So he will turn over the hunts for beaver to us who love the hunt and love the mountain life. Meanwhile, he will live in St. Louis in his fancy house with his new wife and political ambitions and will use his capital to supply our rendezvous, transport our plews to St. Louis, and sell them at a profit. The only hitch is that we must send an express to him by March first saying that, yes, for sure, we want him to send that pack train and telling him where the rendezvous will be.

Now Ashley fills four cups from the jug of whiskey—real whiskey, not awerdenty—that he has by his side.

I decline, but Bill and Davey accept.

I say, "General, I like this idea."

I can see even by the dimming flames that he's pleased.

I go on, "But I'd like for the three of us to talk it over before making a commitment. May we do that?"

"Certainly," says the general. He rises and inclines his head in a half bow as he steps away.

Before Bill and Davey can speak, I ask, "Are you as eager as I am?"

"Yes," they say, almost in one voice.

"You see that he's keeping the sure profit for himself and giving us the risks."

A doubled "yes" again, this time with smiles.

"But we get the fun and he has to live in civilization." Feeling mischievous right now, I call it "civil-lie-zation."

"Yes."

I stand up. "Let me see if there's any coffee left in that pot."

I fetch the pot perched on the edge of the coals of the big fire. It has heft.

I go back, pour coffee into their cups where the whiskey was, and give myself some.

Now we talk about what hunts we want to lead in this first year. Bill and Davey want to go where the plews are plenty, the Siskadee and the Snake River. Those hunts alone should make the express to Ashley a sure thing.

I spread my idea in front of them. I want to travel southwest from the Salt Lake in search of new beaver country. There are rivers and mountain ranges to the southwest, definitely. I don't know how high they are, how good the creeks are, how plentiful the beaver will be.

Further on there is Mexican territory, California. That province is said to have a big north-south range of mountains. I may find beaver there. "That would be new territory for us," I emphasize.

I go on enthusiastically: "On to the north there is the Oregon country. Hudson's Bay Company has been trapping there for at least a decade—why shouldn't we Americans compete? And in the middle of all this may be the Buenaventura River, leading all the way from the Salt Lake to San Francisco Bay. Let's find out if that river's really there."

I am candid with my new partners: "What I'm proposing would be a gamble. We may find a lot of beaver, we may not. I might have to turn back before getting to California, I might not. But if our partnership is to thrive, shouldn't we look for new trapping territory?"

Sublette, who has travelled with me more than Davey, says, "Diah, we know your heart is big to go to California. So go."

Davey echoes, "Go."

I'm glad they said that.

❦

That night in my single blanket I can't sleep. I'm relieved that my partners understand that I'm taking a long chance by going toward California. I'm glad they want me to go anyway.

In the middle of the night I get up and open the journal I've devoted to my maps of the West. At the back is folded a map of all of North America, which I copied from one of the published maps of the continent.

I brush a finger across the page from the Rocky Mountains to the Pacific Ocean and then back. From the northern border of Mexico to the southern border of Canada and back.

I think, *I'm going to explore this. All of this.*

After a while, when the Big Dipper marks the time as halfway between midnight and dawn, I drift off to sleep.

Like a brush fire in a wind, word spreads that I'm headed for California, and plenty of men want to join my outfit. I want Tom Fitzpatrick as companion and clerk, but my partner Davey Jackson has already picked Fitz as his clerk. So I choose Harrison Rogers as clerk, an intelligent, decent, and forthright man if ever there was one. Rogers will be faithful in recording details like a pint or gill of awerdenty issued to one of the men, or not issued. Otherwise I accept into my brigade Silas Gobel, who is rightly called half-horse, half alligator; Abraham LaPlant, who speaks a little Spanish and may be useful if we do cross to California; Peter Ranne, a black man (I think one man should represent the Negro race in the crossing of the continent); plus Arthur Black, Jerry, the kid from the Ree sand bar, Daniel Ferguson, John Gaiter, John Hanna, Manuel Lazarus, Martin McCoy, James Reed, John Reubescan, and John Wilson. So says the list I see in Rogers' journal. But I don't expect them to remain names on a list to me. Some will be sturdy in a fight, some wobbly. Some will be amiable companions on the trail, some sour. I may save the lives of some, and some may save mine. When I look back on this collection of men, they will be a coat of many colors.

Just when I think I have a complete roster for this expedition, Jerry, the kid who got his scalp scraped by a ball back on the sand bar in front of the Ree villages, that kid sidles up to me, shyly, and says, "Captain, I want to go to California."

I say, "I can use more like you."

I tousle the kid's hair. Good kid.

Ahead? I have no idea what's going to happen.

That thrills me.

Chapter Nine

We ride out of rendezvous on August 15, 1826, fifteen men and thirty horses carrying 700 pounds of dried buffalo meat. We're venturing into the unknown—I like that phrase, "to venture into the unknown"—and that meat is a safety measure. But I know we'll need a lot of fresh game to match the dried meat and keep the men going.

We lead the pack horses down the Cache Valley, through the valley of the Salt Lake, and then up the Jordan River to the Utah Valley. Here we meet Utes who, according to their stories, have lived in this pleasant place for hundreds of years.

With the help of Harrison Rogers I spread some gifts on a blanket before several of their principal men—generous gifts, I think—three yards of red ribbon, ten awls, a razor, two knives, a pound of powder, forty lead balls, some arrow points, and half a pound of tobacco. They invite us to sit with them in a lodge. I'm glad—I want to know what the country to the south is like.

Here we speak in signs. Though I am slow with my fingers, I can now carry on a clumsy conversation in sign language. These Utes know white people, they say. The Spanish friars were here three generations ago and said they would build a mission here, but never did. Apparently the friars thought of bringing Catholicism to these people but didn't. Since the friars were here, they say, they have seen only a few white people, men coming from the south or east to trade.

To my frustration, they don't know much about the country immediately to the south. Few buffalo in that direction and no beaver, they say. The question about beaver puzzles them—what would we want with beaver? Yes, there is a river to the south, three or four days travel, but...

From the Utah Valley we strike straight south and after three days come to a shallow river running north. Though we see no beaver sign, I name it Ashley's River. The mountains close by on the west side of the river are dry. The soil along the river is dust that the horses' hooves kick into choking clouds.

Tramp, tramp, tramp. When we stop to eat and sleep, the men are out of sorts. I'm out of sorts too, but try not to show it.

I'm anxious for the men to find game, so that we don't dig deep into the pounds of dried buffalo meat on our pack horses' backs. But in a week beyond the Utah Valley we shoot only one antelope and two rabbits.

Another week downstream the mountains pinch in on both sides and block our passage. I lead the outfit up the mountain on the west side, down, and then south along the base of this range. Now the landscape turns illusionary, the distant mountains a pink haze in the dust. We find water maybe every other day, and a little grass for the horses. It's starvation country, and September heat is no better than August heat.

This no country for beaver. So far my search for peltries to the southwest is a miserable failure. Evening meals are a grumble-fest. Our 700 pounds of buffalo jerky are disappearing.

I say to myself over and over as I go to sleep, "It's bound to get better ahead. It's bound to."

We come to another river, a little brackish, but water nevertheless. I name it the Adams, after the President of our country. Along here one evening we eat the last of the buffalo jerky.

The next day another river flows in, the Santa Clara, and immediately I see an amazing gift at a perfect time—corn and pumpkins on the river bank

I say to myself, "The grace of God."

The Indians who are cultivating these crops live very poorly. Their wickiups are made by arching limbs over to make the shape of a bowl upside down. Then the framework is covered with grass, brush, bark, rushes, reeds, even hides. Yet they grow crops.

I trade from my store of gifts for the corn and pumpkins. The men feast on them like children on a birthday cake.

Me too.

The next day travel gets hard again. This Santa Clara river is no blessing—we have to walk in the river bed. Except for an occasional rabbit, we see no game in ten days of walking wet. Two of my men desert us—I won't give their names. We don't see them again. The other men look at each other with something in their eyes that makes me uneasy.

In my journal October pushes September aside and brings a change: I know this river—it's my friend the Siskadee, come down from many miles above. The Spanish call it the Colorado here, from its red coloring. Now it's a powerful, surging river, with lots of rapids. Because only the river offers water, we have to force our way along the narrow bank.

Now all of us are on foot. Half of our horses have died, and the others are burdened with loads of gear and trade goods.

I'm beginning to think we are like the Israelites wandering in the desert without food or shelter.

Will California be a haven?

⁓

Suddenly we do see a haven. It's several villages on the bank of the Colorado. We can see fields of cultivated crops. As we walk further, grinning at each other, we see that the fields are full of corn, pumpkins, beans, watermelons, and even wheat and cotton.

We will greet these people as friends, for sure. We will give them gifts. And we'll get to eat and drink.

Another hundred steps toward the village I stop for a moment and look across the river. I have a realization: Across this river, that's California.

With my first step on the far bank I will be the first, as far as we know, to cross the continent to California.

Chapter Ten

These people call themselves the Mojave Indians, and they are strange to us. The men wear either just a loin cloth or nothing at all. The women wear only short skirts of bark. The pieces of bark stick out straight about two hand spans behind, to a comical effect.

After I make them presents, they welcome us in a good spirit. I will hold the brigade here for a couple of weeks. I'll trade some horses for stronger ones, and the others can recover on good grass. The men will get better on the vegetables of the fields.

What's best is that these Mojaves know the desert to the west and the missions on the other side. It's not far to the missions, they say, and I'll go there as soon as my men and horses are able to travel.

I want guides across the desert, and the Mojaves have them. Some men have been captured as slaves at the missions. Of these several have run away and come back home. I talk to two of these men and hire them to guide us.

◈

Crossing the desert—I will call it the Mojave Desert in honor of our guides—is painful even in late October. We walk from morning until night, from water hole to water hole, across a country of complete barrens. One day we tramp across the bed of a dry lake, now parched into a plain of white salt glistening in the sun. Nothing makes a man thirsty like a lake that is bone dry.

At last we come to the desert's one pretense at a river. I give it a name, the Inconstant River, for good reason: It alternates between flowing on the surface, and so offering a drink to man and beast, and flowing underground. Where the water is kind enough to rise out of the earth, willows and cottonwoods spring up gratefully. This time of year the cottonwood leaves are not green but gold. We drink and drink, and the horses outdrink us.

At last the river rises into its sources in the mountains that lie to the west. We climb over this range and descend into... paradise.

Chapter Eleven

Here in late November the coastal lands of Southern California are shifting into what is winter in this climate. Small streams lined by trees wander everywhere, and our horses insist on stopping to snatch up the abundant grass. Everywhere within sight scatter herds of horses, cattle, and sheep.

These are the lands and the herds of the San Gabriel Mission, on the Santa Ana River, nine miles west of the pueblo of Los Angeles. With the help of LaPlant, my translator, I soon learn that the full name is Mission of the Saintly Prince the Archangel, St. Gabriel of the Tremblors. With a twist of a smile, LaPlant says that "Tremblors" means earthquakes.

The masters here are Franciscans who are in the process, in their view, of civilizing the native Tongva people and making them Catholics. Civilizing means teaching them to do agriculture, mechanical arts, and the raising and care of livestock. The sheep and cattle, crops, and vineyards keep the tables of the Franciscans nicely supplied with excellent food, wine, and even whiskey. The Tongva people, from what I can observe, adapt well to the new ways they are learning.

Right away we are allowed to share in this sumptuous lifestyle. The Indians slaughter a cow for feasting and add some good corn meal. My men go at the feast with a will.

Soon two friars appear. They ask in Spanish, "May we conduct your leader to the mission?" LaPlant translates.

"How far?" I ask.

First comes a shrug of the shoulders, then, "Walking the horses, about one hour."

LaPlant and I go with the friars, leaving the men to their feast. I suppose I can accept the welcome of the friars. We Methodists are uneasy among Catholics.

At a farmhouse our party is confronted by a corporal. I understand nothing of what he's saying, but his smile says he's trying to put a demand in a polite way. LaPlant translates: I have to surrender my rifle and pistol.

Reluctantly, I hand over my weapons.

I wait for what seems to be a long time, and then a man appears with a written message from the master of this mission, Friar Jose Sanchez. I look at the message and see that it's written in Latin. Stumped, I say, "Please conduct me to the leader of this mission."

That request brings on a long gallop to an impressive, castle-like building with an old man sitting in the portico. My escort indicates that this is the holy father.

I approach him in a gingerly way, uncertain how to introduce myself. Seeing my uncertainty, the padre stands up, extends a hand, and says "Friar Jose Bernardo Sanchez." Then he invites me inside for some cheese and bread. As it turns out, the cheese and bread are accompanied by rum. I take the glass, fidget with it, sip, and keep a straight face. After a look at Friar Sanchez's expectant eyes, I smile, gulp the rest down, and smile again. "Excellent," I say falsely.

Then, having broken my own silence, I explain to the reverend father how I have come to find myself in Mexican territory. LaPlant translates into mellifluous Spanish. "We are hunters of beaver," I say. "We set out from the Great Salt Lake about a hundred days away. Looking for beaver, we walked always to the south and southwest. After many hardships and the deaths of our horses, we arrived at the villages of the Mojave Indians."

Sanchez surely knows about these villages. I wait for a sign of recognition but get none.

I go on, "When I heard that it was not far to this mission, I decided to come here and give my men and horses an opportunity to recruit. Now I will determine the best way to return to my own country, hunting beaver all the way."

I hesitate, but Friar Sanchez just smiles gently. Finally, I conclude, "Two Indians who know the way to the mission guided me and my men here. Now, destitute, we ask for your hospitality."

With LaPlant still translating, the reverend father says that Jedediah's explanation is beyond his understanding. He says, "May I send for an American who lives nearby to facilitate matters?"

No choice. "Yes, Father, I'll wait." A servant shows me to a comfortable bedroom. I relax on the bed.

It's a long wait. Eventually, I'm summoned to meet Señor Martinez, a businessman himself. After we talk, he says we are invited to dinner with the reverend father, which will be very good.

Otherwise, Martinez sees trouble. He says I will have to ask permission of the governor of California to stay in Mexican territory. "You will find it very difficult to make the governor comprehend your business. He has been raised without knowing the hand that fed him as a gentleman, and those Mexican gentlemen know very little about business of any kind, and much less yours. He may detain you here a long time. He will not consider the expense of the wages of your men nor your anxiety to join your partners."

I don't like this. Friar Sanchez is kind, but...

I sit down and write the governor in a tone I hope is more than respectful:

TO GOVERNOR JOSE ECHEANDIA OF ALTA CALIFORNIA

My men and I, fourteen altogether, are simple beaver hunters. We left the Great Salt Lake in August and rode south through a desert county, finding no beaver at all. We suffered greatly as we rode, and our horses suffered more—about half of them died. At last, hungry and thirsty and still hoping to find beaver, we were forced to cross the desert and enter Mexico. Now we are fortunate to enjoy the hospitality of the Mission of the Saintly Prince The Archangel, St. Gabriel of the Tremblors and Friar Jose Bernardo Sanchez.

We have a license to hunt beaver in the land of the United States west of the Rocky Mountains.

We request permission to leave California on our quest for beaver when my men and horses have recovered their vigor. I propose to take my party north toward San Francisco and follow the river that enters the bay there back to the Salt Lake.

Respectfully,
Captain Jedediah Smith

☙

Father Sanchez proves to be steadfast in his generosity to his uninvited American guest, me and every one of us.

Our two Indian guides do not fare as well. They are punished as runaways from the mission. Both are imprisoned, and one sentenced to death. When I plead his case to Father Sanchez, though, the reverend father agrees to pardon him.

Most of the Indians who work at the mission seem happy. They work in the vineyards, orchards, and fields, they make blankets, they produce the wine and whiskey. They seem to have a good life.

And they get on well with my men. The women get on especially well, and often invite the men to bed them. One even asks Harrison Rogers to make a *blanco pickanina* with her. But my clerk is a fastidious fellow. He tells me that because she is so forward, he "has no propensity to tech her."

Soon I'm required to make a trip to San Diego to explain my intrusion into California in person. But my spoken words do no more good than my written words. The governor is suspicious:

"Why are you hunting an animal I never heard of?"

"Captain" Smith—are you on a military expedition into our territory?"

"Captain Smith, your license allows you to have 75 men. Where are the rest of these men? Are they secretly making maps of our province and the placement of our cities?"

I'm not surprised when the governor demands that I go to Mexico City to get permission to stay in California. But I'm disgusted. *Next he'll want me to ask permission to breathe his air.*

At last I appeal to the captains of several American ships in the San Diego harbor. They tell the governor that I really am just hunting beaver, nothing objectionable. On their authority, Echeandia says, "Oh, all right."

But he won't quite get out of our way. We are not allowed, he says, to go north to San Francisco and then east to cross the Chalk Mountains to get back to the Rockies. I must take my outfit back the way we came, across the Mojave Desert.

I ask an American resident who's a friend of the reverend father what the Chalk Mountains are.

He smiles amiably. "A hundred miles north of here a major mountain range rises up. It extends on north for several hundred miles, I don't know how many. The peaks are so high they're covered with snow the year around." Now he adds a twinkle in the eye to his smile. "The Spanish call them the Chalk Mountains because they haven't explored them closely and think the snow is chalk."

I'm non-plussed.

"If you try to cross those mountains," he says, "you may wish they were chalk."

Chapter Twelve

When I get back to the San Gabriel mission in late January, relieved to be set free, I lead the brigade out. First we cross the mountains to the edge of the Mojave Desert. I admit that this start toward the desert is a feint. Immediately we turn north along this edge and cross some other low mountains into what the Californians call the San Fernando Valley. Yes, I'm disregarding the orders of the governor. I'm sick of politicians and politics. I'm after beaver.

We may or may not be in Mexican territory here. I don't know where the Mexicans draw the eastern border of California. There's a big mountain range ahead, and I won't be turned away from beaver.

Riding north, we soon see mountains, probably the Chalk Mountains I was told about. But I give the range the name Mount Joseph on the map in my journal, in honor of Friar Jose Bernardo Sanchez. He was very generous to us, a true Christian gentleman.

I bet these mountains are full of beaver, the first beaver we've encountered since setting out into the Southwest. For sure the men are optimistic. High mountains mean creeks and rivers tumbling out of them, and that means plenty of plews.

As we march north, the country gets better and better, oaks and sycamores along the streams, some beaver, even more elk, antelope, and deer. The Indians we encounter, though friendly, live poorly. They're naked, have no weapons except for occasional bows and arrows, and eat only roots, acorns, and grass. My men fare better for eating, hunting, and trapping as we do.

As April turns to May in my journal, we must be several hundred miles north of San Bernardino, and even farther from the governor. Our horses are piled high with beaver—about 1500 pounds of plews.

These plews make me happy—I'm happy to have a really good hunt—but they're a problem. The rendezvous of 1827 is two months away--how can I get all these plews to the rendezvous, to my partners, and ultimately to General Ashley?

I look up at the mountain barrier to the east. I smile at the illusion of the Mexicans that those vast reaches of white may be chalk. I swallow hard.

I take the brigade over one more set of hills to the next river, a big one, and look east toward the mountain barrier. It doesn't look any less formidable here, but I'm out of choices.

To the devil with it—the job has to be done. We turn up along the canyon toward the summits ahead.

Snow flakes down on us from the skies. The horses flounder and fall down. The men slip to their knees, crunch their faces into the snow, and cuss.

"Goddamn it!"

"Shit!"

By day we're discouraged at tramping through the deep snow. Even in May we worry about freezing to death at night. Soon our horses start showing their ribs again.

I look at those ribs, purse my lips, and order the party to turn around. Still, five horses die before we get back to our companions.

When we stagger into warmth and collapse on good grass, just getting down feels like an achievement.

My journal says it's the middle of May now—six weeks to rendezvous at Bear Lake.

We backtrack by one river. Here's there plenty of game to eat and the horses have plenty of feed.

We get word of trouble. Some authorities at nearby missions are complaining by letter about the band of Americans crossing their lands. Some say we're stirring up the Indians. Others claim we may be mapping the country for a possible invasion.

These gripes reach Governor Echeandia. He issues an order that I must be taken into custody.

꩜

I have a different idea. I'm going to have a try at getting over those mountains again. I made a mistake, I think, in taking the entire brigade first. Now I'll go with just two companions, a few horses, and plenty of food for man and beast. I'm confident the others will be fine here—the governor just wants me.

My big concern isn't as much the mountains as the country beyond us. No one knows what it's like—not my fellow trappers, not the Hudson Bay crews who have roamed over most of the land west of the continental divide, no one. It's probably as bad as the Mojave Desert, but... No one knows—that's pure and simple truth. At least my experience crossing the Mojave taught me how to find water in the desert. I hope for something better than the Inconstant River.

Maybe I can get guides across that desert, but I can't count on that. I don't know what Indians I'll find on the far side of these mountains, whether they'll be friendly, whether they will know a route all the way across to the east side or not—I have no idea. I've learned that often Indians don't know the country just fifty miles away, if the land is forbidding.

Two considerations rule me: I darned well need to stay clear of the governor's soldiers, who want to put me in jail. And I'm determined to get to rendezvous.

Companions? Without saying so, I re-appraise the men I've been with for nearly a year. Silas Gobel seems like a good choice, a bull of a man who can probably lick anyone or anything. Also, Gobel doesn't strut, doesn't boast, doesn't brawl, and doesn't get drunk. He's amiable, cooperative, and quick to catch on. His only defect doesn't matter. He's been in the mountains for four years now and speaks only the trapper lingo—

"This coon don't cotton to no city doin's, no way, no how. Wagh! And he don't want no truck with no man what don't know a Sioux moccasin from a Cheyenne."

I don't speak that lingo, but I understand it.

I also like Robert Evans. He's slender, younger than Gobel, quiet and able to get things done. He reminds me of myself.

First, along with these two, I take one day for hunting, two days drying meat on scaffolds, and a day packing loads on the horses.

Then, after a good dinner of an antelope just killed, time for serious business. I pour coffee from the pot on the coals and call Harrison Rogers aside. I sit on one boulder, my clerk on one a little lower.

When we talk business, we say "Captain Smith" and "Mr. Rogers."

First I pour coffee for each of us. I sip from the steaming cup and say, "Very fine." Sorry, Ma, coffee is a habit with me now.

Rogers sips and says, "Very fine."

"Mr. Rogers, I will set out across the mountains with Gobel and Evans tomorrow morning."

"Yessir."

"While I'm gone—it will be months—stay here with the men. Trap. Scrape hides. Hunt. But unless you are driven away, stay here."

"Yessir."

"If you're forced to move, cache the furs and leave a note saying where I can find you."

"Sure."

I take a long swallow of coffee, fix my eyes on Rogers, and say, "Now this is important. I will be back here by September 20. You'll know the date by your journal."

I pause and then measure these next words out. "If I am not here by that date, consider me dead. In that case proceed to the Russian settlement at Bodega Bay, get supplies, and make your way to the depot." He knows that "the depot" means Cache Valley, home away from home for us trappers.

I plunge on, and this next is important, so I speak with emphasis: "If for any reason you are unable to go to the depot from Bodega, wait for an opportunity to sail to the Sandwich Islands," meaning Hawaii, "and from there to the United States."

Rogers is taken aback. Without a word he reaches out for my cup, steps over to the fire, and fills the cups. Stepping back, he stumbles a little and sloshes some coffee out of my cup. He takes a deep breath, goes back, refills the cup, treads back, hands me the coffee, and sits down.

Finally he says, "I see. I can pay my way at the Russian post with furs. Same with the passages at sea. But I will lose my friend the captain."

Uneasy, he stands up, drains his cup, sets it down, and looks at me squarely. "I understand, captain."

Chapter Thirteen

Tomorrow I will set out with Evans and Gobel to cross these mountains, taking five horses and two mules. The animals will carry hay for themselves and dried meat for us. I'm set on getting back here within four months, by September, in time for the fall hunt. Since I'm taking no plews at all back to rendezvous, that hunt must count. And the mountains here have plenty of beaver—the hunt will be good.

I feel sure of being back here in time.

And my heart is already going further. I'm thinking that during next winter I will march my outfit far north to the mouth of the Columbia River, the heart of the Oregon Territory the British want to coopt for themselves. I will fill my notebooks with maps all the way and bring my entire brigade to the rendezvous of 1828 with a year and a half worth of peltries. If Bill Sublette and Davey Johnson feel let down by my performance in the first year of our partnership, I will come through for them in a big way in the second year.

In the meantime, I will explore, and fill my journal with more maps.

I am very happy. First to cross the continent from the Rockies to California. Then, next winter, north past the Russian settlements to the mouth of the Columbia River, and last, we'll complete the circuit by returning to the Rockies. The entire West will be sketched in my journal.

If I live through all of that.

Well, even then there will still be details to fill in on my maps. That makes me happy too.

※

Starting May 20, 1827, the three of us start up the canyon that has turned the outfit back once. On May 25 we trudge into the mountain's full fury.

In the middle of the afternoon the wind and snow hit us hard. I hurry men and beasts into camp in some pines. "Hobble the horses before they run off," I shout over the wind. I throw down some hay for them.

Gobel gets a little fire going, and we crowd around it, partly to block the fire from the wind. We have a wordless meal of jerked meat. If we had spoken, the wind would have whipped the words off as fast as it sped the heat from the burning twigs away. At first I chafe at the brittleness and chewiness of the meat—and then I'm glad to have it in my belly.

The wind whips at the twigs until they're dead out.

The long twilight brings no relief. The winds get nastier and nastier and by full dark are howling. Our blankets seem to give no more protection than paper would, even when pulled up to our ears. The wind fights the fire and wins. I hear a lot more of "Goddamnit" than I want to hear.

In the middle of the might I get up to check on the animals. Two horses and one mule have frozen to death. Now

Jedediah Smith

I become a doubter—will any of us three men survive the night? Or will we freeze solid where we sit huddled?

On the morning of May 27. I somehow still have eyes to see the gleam of the rising sun on the high peaks. The winds go slack, and the snow stops. Evans gets a good fire going. Gobel says, "Goddamn it, let's start the coffee." The flames warm hands and faces.

At midday the sun rouses us to real comfort and we walk. Unfortunately, we're without two horses and one mule, and almost all the meat they were carrying.

༄

We tramp downhill for about twenty-five miles that day, mostly through light snowfall. We're without the meat carried on the backs of the horses and the mule that died last night. Now another of the horses dies, but the snow stops, and then we come into a little valley with good grass for the remaining animals.

Finally we walk off Mount Joseph, the cursed Chalk Mountains, to a big lake. It's a desert-wrapped stretch of water with some trees and a little grass for the horses and mules still living. We're glad to bed down on warm sand instead of cold snow.

When I look beyond the lake, I have to look quickly at the faces of my comrades. Maybe they've noticed what's out there, but they're not focusing on it.

What I see is trouble, trouble, trouble—flat, barren desert and more flat, barren desert. But as they saddle their mounts and get the animals ready to travel, I don't hear a word of complaint or see a discouraged face.

To get back east to the region of the Salt Lake, we may be faced with a desert like the one like the one I named the Mojave. We're in the same brutal desert, three hundred miles to the north.

I say assuring words to myself: I'm good at finding water holes in the desert, and there can't be that many Inconstant Rivers. I assure myself again and get mounted.

We lead the horses and mules in silence, which is the way I like it. Out in front I keep my eyes peeled for game but see nothing at all. That night, at a dry camp, we eat some more of the dried meat, which is now redistributed to living beasts, and feed the animals hay. We drink half the water in our horns, hoping for a water hole tomorrow. Our animals go thirsty, which makes them restless during the night. We three don't talk—our throats are parched.

All the next day we walk under a hot June sun across nothing but sand, only guessing at the best route. Toward evening I see some dark shapes against the sand and begin to hope. As we get closer, the dark shapes turn green, and I think *cottonwoods!* Yes, cottonwood trees and water, and I'm in it fast. I hold up a hand to tell Sobel and Evans to keep the horses back. This water is waist deep, and I don't want them to soak the dried meat or hay. We've got water—hooray! —but we still need food.

When the horses come up, the three of us have to cooperate at letting the beasts drink without getting in deep. Then we dunk ourselves to the tip-top of our heads, and stand up spouting. When we've fed the horses and mules, fed ourselves, and slept well, we wake up and eat. I tease Evans about being skinny as a scarecrow (the only scarecrow here is me, Diah of the Scary-Scarry Face). He dumps water on my head—we have plenty! —then on Gobel's head, and then his own. In the cool of the dawn, we leave in high spirits.

❧

But the sand still stretches ahead forever and ever. Over the next few days, sometimes we find water, some camps are dry. Mostly we're silent and irritable.

I dream of my family back home. In the dreams we're always at the dining table. In particular I look at the pitcher of iced tea and in the dream help myself aplenty. Surely these pictures parade through me because I'm hungry and thirsty every day.

I also dream of going to church. I see myself in the congregation singing "What a Friend We Have in Jesus." We three are wandering in the desert, in Bible tradition, and we could use a divine friend right now.

Several times we come across Indians. I write in my journal that they again look like "the most miserable of the human race." They're naked and eat nothing but grass, seeds, grasshoppers, and the like. What kind of world have we wandered into?

In the evenings Gobel and Evans talk only of rendezvous, companionship, horse races, shooting contests, and willing squaws.

When I think ahead to rendezvous, I'm concerned. I hope that Smith, Sublette, and Jackson will have lots of plews and be able to pay off our note to General Ashley.

One morning I wake up and give the land we're crossing a name in my journal, the Great Sandy Plain. Occasionally a mountain rises up above the flatness, and a little water trickles down, but it soon sinks into the sand. Game is scarce.

As we walk, we seldom talk and never joke. There's little to say and less to laugh about. Sometimes there's water at the end of a day, sometimes not—we're almost getting used to that. There's hardly ever anything to eat but dried meat.

Then a change: Just when I think the Salt Lake may not be far away, a mountain range rises and runs northeast. We make camp on a little creek that comes off the mountains. I see several antelopes, but I don't get a good shot at any. I do shoot a couple of rabbits. Chomping on the roasted meat, Gobel says, "Better than horse meat."

The next day I lead us down the creek to where it pools into a small lake. We drink and fill our horns with water. Further on we pass some springs too salty to drink. Then we come to some water that is barely drinkable. Frustrated, we pass on, hoping to find better. We end up in a dry camp.

The next morning I tell Evans and Gobel to walk on while I climb a hill for a good look-around. My eyes probe and probe for water, but I see only one chance—a snowy mountain fifty or sixty miles away. Otherwise nothing but the Great Sandy Plain. My heart droops.

When I come down and catch up, Gobel tells me that one of the horses has given out and was left a little way behind. Evans casts his eyes down and won't look up. When I speak, I'm surprised at how scratchy I sound to myself. "Go back and get the best of the horse's flesh," I tell them.

Our supply of meat has dwindled to almost nothing.

While the two are gone, I write in my journal. I describe the desolation I've seen—fifty or sixty smiles of sand stretching between here and that snowy mountain. Damn it! I tell my journal I think it's all right to cuss in extremis.

When Evans and Gobel get back with the meat of the dead horse, they start packing it onto the surviving animals. As I watch, I tell myself that I'm obliged to let them know what I've seen. Fifty or sixty miles of sand! The thought stops my tongue. Again, I'm obligated to tell them, yet I still can't speak up.

I watch the two men—my friends—in their slow, careful movements around camp, hanging their heads. But I can't find it in myself to give voice to how bleak things look ahead—fifty or sixty miles and *then* the snowy mountain.

I consider again. At length I say, "I saw some black at a distance. We're bound to find water near that."

What can we do but push on in search of water? I walk out ahead for a bit and wait until Evans and Gobel come up. Their heads are down, their bodies drenched with sweat. I say what I think I should say: "Probably we will find water, and soon." But all three of us look ahead and see that the situation is almost hopeless.

These are the longest days of the year, around the summer solstice. We push forward, crunching along on soft sand. About four o'clock, with the sun still high, we stop on the side of a sand hill under the shade of a small cedar. We chew on a little meat, which is miserably dry. Now our mouths won't even produce saliva. None of us can scratch out a word.

We sit in that little patch of shade, still not speaking. I get out my journal and write:

> Such walking is very tiresome to men in good health who can eat when and what they choose and drink as often as they desire, and to us worn down with hunger and fatigue and burning with

thirst increased by the blazing sands it is almost insupportable.

I know that's too gentlemanly a way to put it. Worn out by the sun, we dig holes in the sand and lie down in them.

At about sunset I see several turtle doves and point at them. "I've never seen a turtle dove," I begin. My voice sounds so dry I'm angry at it. "I've never seen a turtle dove more than two or three miles from water," I tell them. I try to smile but know it's more like a grimace. I brush sand off myself and go on. "Drain the last drops out of your horns and let me carry them." Then I make myself stand up straight and walk pertly in the direction I saw the turtle doves go.

When I come back, more than an hour later, I hand the empty horns back to my men without a word.

After resting a while longer, we three start our interminable walking again and tramp until ten o'clock at night. Now I think we can probably sleep a little. That is, collapse into sleep.

Though I sleep in the desert, my dreams carry me home. I dream of mother and father, brothers and sisters, fried chicken and mashed potatoes on the dinner table, and iced tea in front of my plate. In the next few minutes I see corn on the cob, fresh green beans, and an apple pie my mother has baked.

I wake up in the middle of the night, reaching for the pie, and look around. Blackness in every direction. Irked at seeing nothing I dreamed of, I mutter. "Damn." I feel bitter about having taken myself so far from what I love, the succor of family, the comfort of hymns and prayers voiced by a like-minded congregation, a region of good neighbors, and fields ripe with bounty. That world felt like it was created by a good God. Not a cussed desert.

Though I don't know what Gobel and Evans may be dreaming of, I consider the thought that they should walk with me now, in the hours of cool and darkness, rather than under the flare of the terrible sun.

I wake my two companions, and they trundle along miserably for the rest of the night. As I put foot in front of foot on the endless sand, I am aggravated by what seem to be the sounds of falling waters in my ears. I probably won't live to hear cooling, running water again.

June 25: This day is one of our longest under the brutal rule of the sun. But we got up this morning and set out across more of the sandy plain, tramp, tramp, tramp. What else could we do?

At mid-morning, though, Robert Evans's body quits. He staggers into the shade of another small cedar and collapses. He tries to say what sounds like "I'm done," but even those words come out as a croak.

Gobel and I sit half in and half out of the little bit of shade and speak what words of encouragement we can.

"You're a good man, Robert," Gobel scratches out.

I think and think and then speak. "Robert, that mountain, the snowy one, it doesn't look far off—I think only three or four miles." I fall silent. Talking hurts my throat. "If we find water there, I'll be back for you."

Evans sort of nods. I can't tell whether or not he has a drop of hope left. Can we leave our friend with no water, nothing to eat, and no hope?

Unable to face up to this prospect, the three of us just sit there. And sit there. When I can stand it no longer, I get up, and Gobel does the same, brushing the sand off his leggings.

I nod at Evans. Then I reach out, shake my friend's hand, and step back, fighting to control my feelings.

Gobel shakes hands with Evans too.

We three look at each other. We have walked a long road together, and have endured together. Now...

Each of us takes a big breath and lets it out.

Without another word I swallow my feelings and lead Gobel into the desert, abandoning our friend Evans.

Chapter Fourteen

At the foot of the mountain we find a spring. Gobel throws down his weapons and powder horn and jumps in all the way, leaning back until the water washes over his face.

I splash it on my hair and my burning forehead, then bury my face and drink until I feel bloated.

As we lie on the edge of the spring, soaked, we see two Indians walking along the rim of a hill in the direction of Robert Evans.

Shortly afterwards we hear two gunshots.

Now we're really fretting about Evans.

Soon after that we see a little smoke in the same direction. Worse and worse.

Feeling amazingly refreshed, I fill a kettle with water and a little bit of meat and head back along the trail.

I find Robert safe. He hasn't seen any Indians, but he fired the shots and built a fire to send up a little smoke—both as a signal to me, "Here I am! HELP!"

I hand my friend the kettle, which holds about a gallon of water, mixed with some scraps of meat. Evans drinks the entire kettle and then complains, "Why didn't you bring more? And why did you bother with the meat?"

In a few minutes he's able to walk as far as the spring.

We three wanderers spend all of the next day at that spring. I use the time to slice up the meat of the dead horse and spread it out to dry under the hammering of the sun.

The next day we walk north along the base of these mountains and come to a lodge of Indians, two men, a squaw, and two children. At first the Indians are nervous about the company of us strangers, who have white skin, dress strangely, and carry long sticks that can kill game at a distance. However, they share their antelope meat with us. More important, they say we will soon be in buffalo country.

When I ask if there's a big lake nearby, they say no.

So I'm surprised the next morning, after another ten miles of tramping, that we come on a grand sight, a vast expanse of water extending far to the north and east. We recognize the Great Salt Lake.

We pound each other on our backs and shoulders. We actually shout aloud, 'Hooray! We did it!' We can scarcely believe that we're so near the end of our troubles. Yes, we're a good way from the depot, but we know we're close to a country where we'll find game and water—and do we ever want plenty of both? 'Hooray!'

I am so excited that I sit down and record the moment:

> Those who may chance to read this at some distance from the scene may perhaps be surprised that the sight of this lake surrounded by a wilderness of more than 2000 miles diameter would excite in me those feelings known to the traveler who, after long and perilous journeying, comes again in view

of his home. But so it is with me for I have travelled so much in the vicinity of the Salt Lake that it has become my home of the wilderness.

Our troubles are not over. Circling the south shore of the lake, we come to the river Jordan, which flows in from Utah Lake. Here in late June the river is still swollen with winter snowmelt. It has overflowed its banks until it's several feet deeper than normal.

We force our way through cane grass to the main channel, which is about sixty yards wide. We look at the current—it's fast.

Studying the river, I have a realization: Most of our pack animals have died along the way—we have one horse and one mule left, and those animals could easily be swept off here and now. We *have* to be careful.

We make a raft out of cane grass and load our possessions onto it.

I tie myself to the raft, saying, "I'll swim it across the river by myself. Animals too."

I push the raft into the Jordan, fighting the current's push against the front end. Then I launch myself and battle the current even harder. I pull the horse and mule along, tied to my mid-section.

After a long struggle, I haul myself, the raft, and the critters onto the far bank. I stamp to get rid of water and shake like a dog. I unload the raft and plunge back in, pushing the empty raft, and swim across to Evans and Gobel.

Now I fix a rope to the raft and put the other end in my mouth. With myself in the lead and Gobel and Evans pushing from behind, we three launch into the river. The current heaves us up, down, and every which way. Before long the rope has wrapped itself around my neck.

I claw at the strangling rope but can't throw it off. Fighting to breathe, I turn toward the raft, heave myself in that direction, and suck in a big gasp of air.

At the same time we're being swept downriver.

I shout to Gobel and Evans, "Harder—swim harder!"

I swim ferociously, and push the raft from time to time to gain enough slack in the rope to get air.

Soon we have drifted beyond where I stashed our gear and supplies. With a desperate last effort, I swim toward the shore. When I feel my toes touching muck, I stand up, and with Gobel and Evans pushing, land the raft.

I throw myself on the ground, work the rope from around my neck, spit out the part I have in my mouth, and lie back, heaving air in.

As I recover, Gobel and Evans load their possessions onto the horse and mule. But then the animals sink so deep into the muck that they're mired.

We fight our way to dry land, pulling the animals. Then we eat a little horse meat and sleep.

The next day we walk down the Jordan River and along the Salt Lake. Our spirits are good: I have told them that within four days we will be in the company of my partners, Jackson and Sublette, and scores of our trapper comrades. Rendezvous—shining times.

On June 30 we forge ahead and feast that night on a fat buck I've shot.

On the first day of July we push on for another twenty miles. The next day we leave the lake and walk into Cache Valley. There we find two hundred lodges of Shoshone

Indians. These people are headed for rendezvous themselves, and say Bear Lake is only twenty-five miles away.

On July 3 we three walk joyfully into rendezvous, trailing two pack animals and no beaver pelts. Our arrival is greeted with great good cheer—the mountain men had given up on our party as lost forever.

General Ashley has hauled a small cannon all the way from St. Louis. Jackson and Sublette ask him to fire it as a salute to us pilgrims.

I listen to the boom and smile, quietly happy.

Chapter Fifteen

This second rendezvous of trappers who come in from all over the mountains and the Indians who do the same is for sure a kind of community. Red and white alike have a good time with horse races, shooting contests, wrestling matches, gambling, and sex.

Sport is the order of the day, beating the other fellow in a foot or horse race, playing cards, shooting at targets, throwing knives into tree trunks, whatever they can think up.

One man beats all. Moses Harris is called Black Harris, maybe for the color of his cheeks, which look like smeared gunpowder. He's a tough hombre, all bone and sinew, with boasts that he can whip any man.

He clears a circle, stands in the middle, and dares all to come at him. The first to hit the ground on his back will be the loser.

Harris throws a lot of trappers and Indians onto their backs and does a noisy dance of victory after each one. Some onlookers say later that Harris threw ten men, and others say twenty or thirty.

But it's all in a convivial spirit. Both white and red have ridden here with good will and for a common purpose—to trade for what they can't get or make for themselves.

General Ashley is the man they line up to talk to. The trappers yearn for coffee, sugar, whiskey, knives, fire steels, lead for balls, blankets, and more. The Indians want the same plus treats for their women to make themselves beautiful—vermillion for their faces, beads, calico, blue cloth, red cloth, ribbon, silk, and trinkets.

Times have changed. At first Ashley hired these men at a fixed annual salary to trap beaver in his brigades, skin the critters out, and deliver the pelts to the general. Now they're on their own. They can trap anywhere they please. In the far north there are plenty of plews but trouble with the Blackfeet. To the northwest a lot of plews but competition with the brigades of the Hudson's Bay Company. The front range of the Rockies are good territory, and so is the Siskadee, though they'll find lots of their brethren wanting to trap the same creeks. Also, they'll have to judge Indian danger for themselves. After Ashley's big mistake at the Ree villages, they may prefer their own judgement.

Ashley now is in the seat of power. He has lots of the supplies, and he's the only seller. He's paying three dollars a pound for plews—three dollars in trade at his prices, not in cash. Two pounds of beaver will get a man three pounds of powder, six pounds of lead, four pounds of coffee, or two pounds of tobacco. Eight pounds of plews will buy the entire lot.

When showing his buddies how much he got for his plews, the trapper will speak of himself in mountain-man lingo— "This hoss done got enough lead to bring down a herd of buffler." Or "This child got enough vermilion to seduce the entire female population of the Sioux nation." Or maybe "This hoss is rich with tobacco—I says *rich*."

Wagh! Plenty of trappers complain about Ashley's prices. Maybe they're a little steep, but the general has traveled many a mile and paid a lot of money to get the goods here. And the mountain men gripe like little old ladies.

Still, this new arrangement is working well—a pack train laden with supplies to the mountains in mid-summer and a pause in trapping to hand over peltries and get re-supplied, talk to old compañeros again, and catch up on all the news all over the mountains—"I'm still above grass, ain't I?" to "Old Jim done lost his hair."

Ashley likes this set-up, I like it, my partners like it, a herd of beaver men like it, and the Indians love it.

◈

When the fun and business of rendezvous are over, I head to California. This time my brigade is eighteen men, including one of my two companions on the brutal hardships of the Great Sandy Plain, Silas Gobel. However, Robert Evans, the man I had to rescue after he collapsed, has decided he's through with this life and is headed back to the settlements with Ashley's outfit.

Among the others in my brigade are a mulatto, a "Spanyard," two Canadians, and their squaws. We mountain men are a motley crew, and we don't care what your color is or where you come from—we value you for what you can *do*.

Now our mission is to pick up the men left at the base of Mount Joseph, head north along coastal California to the mouth of the Columbia River in the Oregon country, and turn east to trek to next summer's carnival. We will trap all that way.

I like trapping and love exploring.

I'm hoping for a good season catching beaver this fall in California and another good hunt next spring in Oregon. That will set me up to bring a big load of plews to the rendezvous next year, send Ashley home happy, and make sure the firm of Smith, Jackson, and Sublette is profitable.

I'm optimistic.

✦

I lead the outfit south and west basically along the route I followed last year, avoiding its worst sections, and at length come to the Colorado River, the old Paiute farmer, and his welcome fields of corn.

Now our route will be down the Colorado River—plenty of water all the way—to the villages of the Mojave Indians, our friends of last year. I haven't forgotten that they provided us with the two guides who led us across the Mojave Desert, up the Inconstant River, and over the mountain to San Bernardino Mission and the great generosity of Father Jose Sanchez.

The Mojave Indians welcome us back again. I set my camp on a spot along the river with good grass. From here I will launch our party across the river and into the challenge of the desert. I make the chiefs some presents, trade a few horses with them, and sit down with Francisco, one of last year's two guides.

News: Since our visit last year, a party of American and Spanish trappers has come along the Gila River to these villages. Here they split up, some of them heading up the Colorado, the rest in some other direction.

I get it—there's competition out of the Mexican provinces. Well, I will trade with the Mojaves for some food—melons, beans, corn, wheat, and dried pumpkin—and get on to California. Since I know the route now, I don't need Francisco to guide us. And I'll worry about Governor Echeandia when we get there.

We stay with the Mojaves for three days, build rafts of cane grass, and load the rafts with our gear. Then I set out with half of the men into the strong current of the river.

∽

Instantly the Mojaves curdle the skies with their war whoops and attack my men left on their side of the river.

Within a couple of minutes, as the current sweeps me and the others away, all nine left there are killed and the two women captured. Silas Gobel lets out a memorable roar as he falls.

I see our dilemma right off. Half of my brigade is still alive, with only five rifles, their butcher knives, and the poles we're using to shove ourselves toward the other bank. We have no horses, and only the dried meat in our possible sacks. Mojave warriors are clustered on both banks, ready to attack.

If we manage to escape immediate slaughter, the nine of us will have to walk across a hostile desert with no horses, meat only for a few meals, and very little water.

Damn Francisco! Maybe the Mojaves had trouble with the previous white-man party and they're taking it out on us. Whatever the issue was, Francisco could have warned me.

I think I remember last year's trail well enough to find the springs that dot the route. As we land on the far bank, though, it doesn't look like we'll get beyond right here.

I look across the river at my dead companions and down the river at several hundred Mojave warriors on this side. They're going to close in and put an end to all our thoughts of the future.

"Leave some of your gear on the sand bar," I tell the eight men still with me. "Take what you want most and can carry." I hope the Mojaves will waste time quarrelling about who gets to keep what.

Now I get my little outfit into a small thicket of cottonwoods, and it's time to get the men to brace up.

"Lop off some of the small trees," I say, showing them how. I clear enough space for us to cluster in. "Then cut off the tops."

I demonstrate.

"Now fix your knives like this." I lash my butcher knife to the hefty end of the tree trunk, blade forward.

"That makes it a lance," I say, jabbing the air.

Not much of a lance, I think, *but better than being empty-handed.*

"Now we wait for them."

I appraise our situation. More Mojave warriors are gathering on the bank downstream. If they want to, they can attack from three directions, every side but the river.

I look around and confirm it: My eight men have only five rifles, including mine. I note the two best marksmen in my mind. If we get rushed from one side, I'll hold the shots down to those two and myself. No sense in letting all five of us fire at once, so that we'll all be reloading when the Mojaves rush us.

One of the men says, "Captain, do you think we can hold them off?"

Hell, no! I think. But I say, "Yes, I think we can."

The Mojaves edge closer and closer. It won't be long.

Then I see that some of the bolder warriors have ventured out into the open. They're within long range for a shot.

I tell Bo'sun Brown and Isaac Galbraith to take shots when they're certain—certain! —of killing. And I level my own Hawken.

Three blasts sound, almost as one.

I see two Mojaves fall, surely dead. One is crawling back toward his comrades.

And then a miracle: The Mojaves run off like frightened sheep. Maybe, like many tribes, they regard a fight in which they lose even one man as a defeat.

Chapter Sixteen

When twilight comes, we slip away into the desert. After a long night of walking, we come to a spring. Since the sun and heat cut like blades and we have no way to carry water, we stay beside the spring until the next twilight.

During the night we move east, but in the darkness I lose my way. I curse a hard fact: I've come along this route only once, and my memory is spotty. At dawn I climb a hill and see another hill in the distance in the direction I want to go.

OK. I pick one man to walk with me, Galbraith. "The rest of you," I say, "if we don't come back, walk toward that big rock sticking up."

Galbraith and I go forward, following either my instinct or my nose for water, I'm not sure which.

We find it. Worn out, I send Galbraith back to bring the others up and collapse into sleep.

When the crew arrives, I climb another hill and see that we're about five miles to the right of last year's trail and opposite a water hole I remember.

We rest until sundown and then start tramping again. I urge them on until mid-morning, when we find a spring. We fill our bellies repeatedly and rest all day and all night.

Then I take a chance. Last year our guides pointed out a short way across the barren desert to the Inconstant River, but they said it was too rocky for horses. Now we have no horses.

That stretch turns out to be brutal. The wind dries our faces, and the sun slashes at us. Our lips split. In our minds we see fantasies of water falling over rocks and splashing into tempting pools.

Now I show the men the juice inside a cabbage pear. They hack open these cactuses and suck on the meat, bitter-tasting but wet.

"Come on, let's go, let's go," I urge, again and again.

As the sun angles down, one man pitches forward into the sand face first. As though prompted, another man falls down beside him.

"I'm dizzy," says the first.

"I'm sick at my stomach," says the second.

"I ache."

"All over."

"I can't get up."

"I couldn't never take another step."

I kneel between them. "Try," I say, "you have to try."

Moans, moans, and more moans.

Now all of us are huddled around the fallen.

"A little way on there's a sink," I say, "with a spring at its edge."

A groan from one, a head shaking NO from the other.

"Just walk a little farther."

"No-o-o," from both.

So I have to explain. "I don't have any water to leave with you."

A chorus of grunts.

"It makes no sense to leave food."

Silence.

"I don't see much chance if I leave you behind."

Silence and more silence.

OK, nothing to be done about this.

"When we find the spring, I'll send water back. Sundown is"—I look at the sun—"in an hour or so. Follow our trail then, if you can." And I point in the direction where I think the spring is.

No sounds from the prostrate men.

I stand up. Then the other six and I walk away.

Every man hates to leave the two. But each one is also agonizing about saving himself.

I'm worried about saving the lot of us. Send water back? Seems doubtful. It might be dark by the time we reach the dry lake. How will I find the spring in the dark? Even the men still on their feet—will they make it that far?

We drag ourselves to the edge of the sink at dusk. I can't remember where the spring is. Then, walking into the last of the sun, I stumble straight onto it. Mountain luck.

Every man charges into the water. We drive our heads into the liquid and slurp it up. We sit down in the water. We soak buckskins and human skin. After a little while our parched tongues make words.

Soon two of us say they're going back to help their comrades. They fill a kettle and set out into the early darkness.

They find the two who gave up, and they are still giving up. The rescuers pour water all over them.

After a while the four stagger up to the spring, waving empty kettles.

The next morning we set out along my old friend the Inconstant River. This so-called stream still runs, or crawls, below the ground for maybe a half mile at a time, then surfaces into a puddle, and then dips underground again. We measure our lives by puddle, now another puddle, now another...

Before long we bump into a group of Paiutes and—miracle of miracles—are able to trade our knives, fire steels, and other paraphernalia for a little food, two horses, and some jars for carrying water.

From there I can see a pass, a way over the San Bernardino Mountains and to the luxurious grass, water, and vast herds of the San Gabriel Mission. It will be a haven, unless Governor Echeandia turns it into hell.

Chapter Seventeen

When we're among the mission's herds of cattle, I count on Friar Sanchez's generosity without asking—we slaughter several beeves, and we feast. Having feasted, we dry some meat. We're back in the land of plenty.

That afternoon I write to Father Sanchez that I had not intended to come back but that an Indian attack had crippled my party. I didn't explain that my plan had been to turn north where the desert meets the San Bernardino Mountains and work my way along the Chalk Mountains—Mount Joseph—to meet the rest of my outfit. Now I feel some urgency to get moving. It's already September, and I told my clerk, Harrison Rogers, to consider me dead and go on without me if I'm not there by September 20.

After recruiting for a few days, we start north without Thomas Virgin, who is suffering from his wounds, and Isaac Galbraith, who is taken with the climate of Southern California and wants to stay.

My outfit and I—we six men can't be called a brigade—head north through what is called the San Joaquin Valley to the river where I left my other men. On September 18 we ride into their camp.

The first words out of Harrison Rogers's mouth are, "Wagh! What a sight for these here eyes! I'd given up on ye!"

That evening all the men party, but they're restricted to celebrating with coffee. Awerdenty? From me? Not a chance.

I hear a couple of men murmur amiably about "Parson Smith," but they won't say it to my face.

༄

The men I left at the foot of the Chalk Mountains in California had a good summer. No Indian trouble. Deer, elk, and antelope as thick as huckleberries in season. Some Spaniards rode out from their settlements and asked some questions but seemed to understand when Rogers told them the outfit was just stuck there.

Thinking of trading the plews I left here all summer, I take several men and ride to the nearest mission.

And into a nightmare.

The friar of the mission takes our horses, makes me and the men go hungry for two days, and then orders us to wait until word can go to Governor Echeandia, who is now headquartered in Monterey. The Friar is suspicious—these Americans, who are undoubtedly apostates, are they trying to sway the Indians away from the one true faith?

I'd gotten fed up with the governor last year. "Your Excellency, I am but a humble beaver hunter..." with a lot of bowing and scraping. And what I got in return was more Suspicion, again with a capital S. Are these men the avant garde of a military mission that will seek to wrest California from Mexican rule?

My men and I are sent under guard to Monterey and clapped in jail. Then the governor brings me before him for questioning: Why did you come back? Why did you use a route you told me was almost impassable? Why didn't you come straight across to your brigade instead of going the long way around via San Bernardino? Why didn't you write me from San Bernardino to inform me of your arrival?

I explain my rescue mission, to no avail. The governor deems all this very suspicious. I will have to go to Mexico City and explain to a higher authority.

This is galling. It would take months for me to travel to Mexico City and be held there for judgment. Meanwhile my brigade would be stuck where they are, and my partners would have to do without the bounty in beaver my men have trapped.

Nevertheless, I say, "I will leave immediately on a British ship."

"Good," says the governor— "You will pay your own expenses."

"Pay my own way to jail?" I protest. "No, no, and no."

"Then wait for a Spanish ship," says the governor, "two or three months from now."

I'm exasperated. "I refuse to go."

I send an appeal to local American residents and ask them to enlist the help of the captains of any American ships in port. There are four and they're glad to help.

They tell Echeandia that they have the authority to represent their government in such a situation, and assure him that I am simply a beaver hunter far from home.

I can see that the governor is reluctant. He doesn't like this. It's a way out of trouble, though. He hesitates, then decides he'll take their word. However, he insists that I must leave California immediately—and he names a route that is completely impractical.

I'm fed up. I ride back to camp and write to the governor and the American embassy in Mexico complaining about the unnecessary suspicions and arbitrary behavior of politicians and their failure to understand business and its necessities.

Now. My men and I have labored for a year and a half with little to show for it. All right, I will take matters into my own hands. With the money from the sale of our plews I will buy three hundred horses. California is overrun with horses—the Spaniards actually drive wild horses into pens and let them starve to keep them off mission pastures. These animals will be worth twenty thousand dollars at rendezvous, a bonanza for Smith, Jackson, and Sublette.

So I will move my brigade out, driving the horses. I'll get out of California for good.

After forced inaction of three and a half months, we start on December 30. That evening I write in my journal:

> Having been so long from the business of trapping and so much perplexed and harassed by the folly of men in power, I return again to the woods, the river, the prairie, the camp with a feeling somewhat like that of a prisoner escaped from his dungeon and chains.

Chapter Eighteen

Unfortunately, because of winter rains northern California is a quagmire. Every low spot is a marsh or a lake. Actual rivers are high, and I'm lucky not to lose a horse crossing several of them. We move only to find new grass.

Stuck, I decide to send my crew into the mountains for beaver. They come back with nearly a hundred plews in a week.

I keep trying to move on. The problem is that the rain is turning the country into a slough. When we try to cross any water, men and horses get covered with mud. Things get worse when two men desert, taking eleven traps with them.

I'm mad. Fewer traps mean fewer beaver.

Soon we meet some friendly Indians who trade some salmon for tobacco. For the most part the Indians we encounter are willing to trade with us. Occasionally, they're hostile and we have to drive them off.

The country is full of deer, so the men have plenty to eat, but California is an endless quagmire.

In April we get into the low mountains of northern California. The firm footing is better than muck, but steep hillsides and deep ravines make tough going. Two horses get pushed off a cliff and killed. Everywhere are bad passages through steep, stony mountains.

May is a relentless sequence of similar miseries. I try to follow the Klamath River, and here I nearly accomplish what the governor demanded—GET OUT OF CALIFORNIA. However, I'm crossing not into the desert of Nevada but into Oregon Territory, which is jointly held (and disputed) by Great Britain and the United States.

Now Harrison Rogers is so distressed at our general predicament that he writes a prayer in his journal and shows it to me:

> Oh! God, may it please thee still to guide and protect us, through the wilderness of doubt and fear. Oh! Do not forsake us, Lord, but be with us, and direct us through.

The scramble from central to northern California has held us up for five months, and nature has been harsher even than the politicians.

While South California entranced two men into staying, Northern California is yelling, GET THE HELL OUT!

❧

Frustrated with the mountains, I head us for the beach. Getting there turns out to be tough. Fog puts a stop to visibility. The game seems to have disappeared, and the men miss what they do shoot at. Though the Indians trade us mussels, eels, fish, and berries, the men don't like this fare. Before we get to the ocean, we kill a young horse and feast. Then I get lucky and shoot three elk. The men gorge on the meat, raw.

Though I thought the beaches would be better travelling, they aren't. Some are stony, others covered by high tides. The tidal rivers are hard to cross—too deep. We lose some of our horses in the Rogue River—too many of the three hundred crowd into the river at once. That makes a dozen lost in a few days.

It's about the first of July now, and rendezvous is getting started. We're going to miss it completely, but I can't think about that. Instead I have to cope with big rivers that force us upstream to find a ford.

One form of relief: These Kelawatset Indians are used to trading with the British at Fort Vancouver, and so understand my proposals to trade. Also, the Kelawatsets say they know of a passable route to the valley of the Willamette River to the north.

Now a bit of trouble: An Indian steals an axe. LaPlant and I grab the thief and demand to know where the axe is. At the same time our other men point their rifles at a big bunch of Indians. The thief shows us where he has buried the axe in sand.

But we've made a mistake. This thief is a chief, and he is mortally insulted. Back in the village he cries out for vengeance but is overruled by another chief.

Two days later I leave the brigade at the forks of the Umpqua River to scout ahead for the best route, as I usually do. I go in a canoe with John Leland, Sumner Turner, and an Indian guide.

Leaving, I tell Harrison Rogers not to let any Kelawatsets into camp while I'm gone. Though I myself sometimes let Indians into camp, I don't trust these Kelawatsets—there are too many of them and they're volatile.

But Rogers lets the Kelawatsets into camp anyway. Why not? They have good relations with other whites.

The peace-making chief of a day or two earlier mounts and rides proudly around camp. Arthur Black sees him and thinks this is too much arrogance.

"Hey, you there, get down."

He takes the chief's reins and holds them. "Down," he yells, "down." With one hand he points emphatically to the ground.

Offended, the chief dismounts. But now a second chief has been humiliated and outraged.

The Indians watch the white men until they see them drying their guns from yesterday's thunder shower.

Now they attack.

Two men grab Arthur Black's gun and wrestle him for it. They slice at his hands with their knives until he loses his grip. He sees an axe swinging toward his head, jumps aside, and takes the blow of the axe on his back.

He sprints for the woods. Taking a quick look behind, he sees nothing but axe blades swinging and trappers falling.

༺

Black stumbles through the forest in a daze. His mind fights him, but he forces himself to remember what he has seen. He reels. He falls. He slips toward sleep, but he's shaking with terror, and that keeps him awake. He staggers around, helpless.

After several days he stumbles down to the ocean. His mind is clearing. He will have to get to Fort Vancouver and beg for help. He has no horse and no rifle, and the fort is about a hundred miles away, but he has no choice.

Several days north along the coast he runs into some Indians who strip him naked and take his knife. He doesn't give a damn—he keeps walking north.

Later he blunders into some Tillamooks, and they guide him to the fort.

When Black gets to Fort Vancouver, almost four weeks after getting chased into the woods by the Kilawatseks, he is incapable of speech. John McLoughlin, the factor, sits him down and talks to the horror-struck man until he comes around. After a while Black, though still incoherent, gets the words out:

"I am the only survivor of the massacre of the brigade of Jedediah Smith. Smith and all the others," he stammers, "uh, they have been, uh, murdered. Murdered, uh, by the Kilawatseks on the, uh, Umpqua River."

⁕

The following morning McLoughlin sends native runners to the Indians of the Willamette to ask them to bring in any white men still living. The following day, as a party of trappers is setting out on the same mission, Tillamooks come in with me, Leland, and Turner.

So now I get the story from Black. Fifteen men have been murdered, plus an Indian boy. All the plews are gone, and all the horses—everything I hoped to take back to my partners as the yield of two full years of effort.

I retreat to a quiet place. I'm obliged to remember them one at a time: The pious Rogers, who was so offended by a senorita's forwardness that he declined to touch her. The black man, Ranne, who suffered in recent days from swelling in his legs. Thomas Virgin, the old man I'd been so glad to see after the elder got out of the Spaniards' prison. Marechal, Swift, Palmer, Reubescan, Lapoint, McCoy, Gaiter, and LaPlant, my translator. Lazarus Daws, and even Marion, the Tillamook boy I recently saved from slavery.

I've gone hungry and thirsty with these men, tramped across barren desert with them, yarned with them across a fire, and spread my blankets next to theirs. They were comrades.

Now all are dead.

I'm sick at heart.

And mad as hell.

Chapter Nineteen

I'm lucky that Dr. John McLoughlin is the factor at Fort Vancouver, the post of the Hudson's Bay Company. At six feet, four inches, with a big shock of hair that's prematurely white, McLoughlin is an imposing man. And though an employee of the Hudson's Bay Company, he is humanitarian enough to be generous to all comers, British, French-Canadian, American, and Indian. Now I benefit from that generosity.

McLoughlin himself is about to send a brigade south, led by Alexander McLeod. The doctor offers me and my three men, Black, Leland, and Turner, the opportunity to join McLeod's outfit. We certainly couldn't get our property from the Kilawatseks on our own, or avenge our comrades. We join McLeod gladly.

Within a few days we're less glad. A rider brings a letter from McLoughlin saying that our property is scattered all over and chances of recovery are poor. On the other hand, McLoughlin writes that if the massacre goes unpunished, the barbarians will feel free to maraud and plunder as they please. In that case, he says, "our personal security will be endangered."

So McLeod rides on with twenty-two Hudson Bay *engagés*, fourteen Indians, and us four Americans. Word in the mountains is that the Kelawatsets are waiting cheerfully to massacre us.

The first Kilawatsets we see run off. But the Indians with McLeod venture out and talk to those who have fled. After some conversation they send their elderly chief in for a sit-down session. The old man asks in a forthright way, "Do you white people want to wage war?"

"No," says McLeod, "we've come to make peace and get the property of Mr. Smith back."

The old man considers and then says, "I will return soon."

That evening, as McLeod and I drink coffee at a good fire, the chief brings in thirty-four of my mules and horses.

"Good," says McLeod. "Sit with us." He offers the old man coffee, putting lots of sugar in it first. The chief smiles and accepts.

McLeod looks at me. I shake my head, meaning no, the horses are not enough.

McLeod says, "These animals—this is not good enough. We want..."

His eyes ask me.

I say evenly, "We want our peltries, our guns, and whatever else was stolen."

The chief finishes his coffee in one swig, sets the cup down, and tells us white men, "Come to the village at the first bend down the river. The day after tomorrow," he says, "when the sun first comes up."

Our outfit rides into the village on that morning in a driving rain and rides out half a day later with six hundred beaver pelts, eight rifles, and a miscellany of knives and other gear.

I tell McLeod to take his brigade on—I will catch up. McLeod considers, nods, and leaves without another word. He understands.

❧

I wander among the skeletons, or bodies, whatever I should call them. I find the torn remains of fifteen of my missing men. The scavengers have taken their turns at my friends—coyotes, crows, bugs, worms...

I look at the ruined faces with revulsion. These men have grown up with parents, brothers, and sisters who still love them. Have been teenagers excited by life, young men thrilled at the prospect of going west. They have enjoyed living, even the mental swirl of one drink too many or the touch of an enthusiastic woman. They have thrilled to the danger of running their horses in a mad herd of buffalo on stampede. They know the delights of living sunrise to sunset and all the nights through.

How alive they were.

Now...

I wander. Their faces are unrecognizable, but some...

I recognize Jerry from his shock of red-gold hair with the scar still showing. Jerry flipped the coin of life and death on that sand bar in front of the Ree villages. The bullet glanced off the barrel of his rifle, gouged out two inches of his scalp and hair, and sailed away. Now he has flipped that coin again and died.

I recognize Reed, a quiet, genial fellow, his tongue stilled forever. Ranne, the black man who has now achieved the full human equality of death. Ranne looks like he was screaming, and his head has been bashed in from behind.

Nepassang, an Indian whose tribe, the Nippissing, has been doing fur trapping for years. He was a worthy hand.

I recognize my clerk, Harrison Rogers, who recorded every transaction we made, every deduction or dispensation, from payment of salary to giving a ration of awerdenty. Big-hearted Rogers was kind, and didn't deserve the payment a war club gave him.

And now I get a twist in my chest. I instructed Rogers not to let the Kilawatsets into camp. But I know from Arthur Black that Rogers disregarded this instruction. Too many Kilawatset warriors got into camp. At a shout from one they all attacked. Unready, all fifteen men died in the swarm.

But I can't be angry at Rogers. What I feel is too big, too overwhelming for anger. I move around, look at bodies, and am swamped with indescribable emotion.

I step a little away and sit where I can, at the bottom of an ocean of sorrow.

Eventually I get up, follow the trail of McLeod's outfit, and rejoin the living.

⁂

Back at Fort Vancouver McLoughlin keeps up his generosity. Though his firm has sacrificed their fall hunt to helping me retrieve as much as possible of my property, the doctor buys my furs and horses at full price.

Now I want to get back to business. I've heard from McLoughlin that my partner Davey Jackson is conducting a hunt near Flathead Post, well up the Columbia River. Since two of my last three men have quit, only Arthur Black and I set out on March 2, 1829, headed up the Columbia by boat, bound for Flathead Post, to the north among the Flathead people. There we get word that Jackson is trapping some distance up the Flathead River.

It's easy to find Jackson and his outfit along the river. I guide our canoe to the bank. As the evening sun goes down, I get out and walk toward the big fire with an uneasy feeling. Davey is my partner, and a stalwart one—over the last three years he has brought in the most fur of the three partners. And Davey is my friend. All that mountain men do—catch beaver, skin them out, run and shoot buffalo, trade with Indians, fight when necessary—he and I have done these things shoulder to shoulder.

But while Davey has brought in a lot of money for our partnership, I have not. The first year, when I crossed to California, I brought in none. I missed the rendezvous of 1828 completely. Now I've lost fifteen men to Indians and been robbed of everything I had.

Yes, I've recovered our some of our furs, horses, and other belongings. Yes, John McLoughlin has given me a good price for my plews and the animals.

But my emotions are soiled. Fifteen dead men haunt me every step of the way.

The issue isn't that those men's families will have to be compensated for the loss of their lives, not at all. It's that...

The first responsibility of a brigade leader is the lives of his men. I failed.

I'm not demonstrative in my friendships. Davey and I greet each other with a clap on the shoulder and "Good to see you, partner."

We sit, we drink coffee, we eat, and Davey gives me his news, which is a lot more upbeat than mine. After rendezvous last summer our partner Bill Sublette took our furs down to St. Louis and sold them for the good price of six dollars a pound. Now he's spending the winter in St. Louis, planning to come back to rendezvous 1829 with the pack train. And Robert Campbell, one of my two great Irish friends, is leading a fur campaign for us east of the divide. That country should have a good yield.

The partnership of Smith, Jackson, and Sublette is healthy.

Davey also has stories of this fellow and that fellow. Jim Bridger can stretch any story beyond belief—he's been known to spin the wildest yarns in the mountains. He's also admired as an unstoppable foe of the Blackfeet.

Bridger was the champeen, says Davey, of yarn-spinning at the last rendezvous. The way Jim told it, "Some Blackfeet run me into a box canyon. I've lost my knife. My rifle and pistol, they's empty. There's no way out, and the Blackfeet is almost on top of me."

Now Jim pauses to let the tension mount. Finally one of the listeners can bear it no longer.

"What happened, Jim?"

"Well, them Injuns kilt me. Scalped me, too."

Tall tales are good sport in the mountains.

Davey and I finish one kettle, make another, and drink all of it, talking, talking, talking.

My spirits lift.

Well, they lift part way. When I roll up in my blankets that night, thoughts of my lost men—some lost on the Colorado River, some lost on the Umpqua—disturb me. My dreams are sodden with death.

Chapter Twenty

Davey and I travel steadily along the west side of the continental divide to a beautiful spot on the back side of the Grand Tetons called Pierre's Hole for rendezvous 1829.

Bill Sublette, Davey, and I now consider. Some hard times are past, the three years of my roam of the entire Southwest and the Northwest. But the troubles I had were offset by good hunts of the other two and my friend Robert Campbell. Our young company has paid its debts and has about $28,000 in the bank. Divided over three years, that's not a lot of profit, and the estates of the men we've lost—I've lost—still have to be paid.

My explorations have brought plenty of information but not enough beaver. Now it's time to concentrate on the best beaver country we know, and we know the mountains better than anyone. Sublette and I will go to the Three Forks of the Missouri. That country bristles with hostility from the Blackfeet, who have plagued beaver men for two decades. Which means that Bill and I will take a strong brigade and be on guard all the time. I will be the booshway. We'll make an armed march—avoid Blackfeet, take beaver, drive off Blackfeet, take beaver.

I insist on military discipline. The brigade moves in a long file. Hunters and scouts ride ahead on each flank, watching for game and for Indians. Then I come, at the head of a long column. I lead the mule that carries the company records, and behind that mule tread a line of pack animals, watched by camp tenders. Then file the trappers, each leading another horse or two loaded with gear. Behind them walk knots of squaws and children, bringing along their belongings by travois. Last comes Sublette, looking out for our rear.

This column of armed men will make even the Blackfeet think twice, or three or four times. As captain I keep everyone, including the horses, in a close-knit group at night. Our trappers are at risk only when out working their traps solo.

In the evenings I sit quietly with my conflicts. I miss life back in the settlements, around people who speak better English, have better morals, and go to church. But around our campfires I have to listen to trappers make fun of the ways of people back on God's side of the Missouri River. People back there still think the Great American Desert on their maps is uninhabitable. They don't know that buffalo run all over those plains, meat on the hoof. They think the Rocky Mountains can't be crossed, yet we mountain men have danced the fandango back and forth over those mountains and even rolled wagons across South Pass. Folks back in the settlements can't read sign to save their scalps, which they will therefore lose when they get here. Read sign? Bill Sublette or Jim Bridger could come on an Indian trail and tell you how many men were on it, from what tribe, whether they were peaceable or warlike, how long ago they passed here, and where they were going.

And people on the wrong side of the Missouri think parsing letters into words and sentences is a big deal.

On and on our men have fun mocking God's side of the Missouri River. Back there they have preachers to tell you how wrong about everything you are and quote Bible words to prove it. Out here you aren't judged by your color or whether you can read and write, what kind of family you come from, or how much money you have, but by your mountain skills and your willingness to stand by your partner. Back there they have sheriffs who boss people around and lawyers to trick you into jail or out of money. People stay in line, especially the churchy line. No one is wild, no one is free, no one goes just whatever direction his gee-whillikers point him. No one knows what it feels like to ride your cayuse in the middle of a huge herd of buffalo, hooves thundering-thundering-thundering, and turf flying past your head.

Who wants to live in such a place?

I listen to this talk and feel swish-swash. I feel the call of the wild. If I see a mountain peak, I want to stand on it and look into country new to human eyes. When I see a beautiful river, I want to paddle it. When I imagine a far shore, like California's, I want to walk until I get there and look across the ocean to infinity. I want to go, go, go, and see, see, see.

And I respect the skills of the men who live out here. They do shoot center. That shot will save your life from an enemy or bring meat for the fire. They know how to make friends with Indians and trade with them instead of fighting them. They know how to make a beaver come to medicine. They will stick by you and stick by you for good.

Yet in my eyes they also have faults aplenty. They fornicate. They get drunk. They speak a version of English so crude it's nearly a foreign language. They are, in a word, sinners.

And I am a Methodist.

※

When I wrap up the fall hunt, I lead the brigade east toward the Yellowstone River. But the Blackfeet can't let us trappers march into their territory and come out unscathed. They mount a full-scale attack.

Though none of our men is killed, they get scattered all over the place.

Joe Meek gets cut off entirely. Stranded with just his mule, blanket, and gun, he decides to make straight for the winter camp agreed on, along the Wind River. Leaving the mule, he sets out southeast and thereby wanders into the hot springs region of the Yellowstone country. The whole area is sending up smoke from boiling springs—he can feel the heat, and he can smell the burning gases. The place reminds him, by God, of Pittsburgh.

Before long I send two trappers out to hunt for Joe, and they bring him back to the brigade. He allows as how he'd thought maybe he'd been near the back door to hell, but "If it war hell, it war a more agreeable place than I had been in for some time."

Now we trap our way up the Big Horn to where the Popo Agie flows in and the Big Horn changes its name to the Wind River.

Winter camp. We build lodges. Shoot buffalo and dry the meat.

And I sit down to do some serious thinking.

Long days in camp, longer nights in the darkness. I have been in the mountains for eight years now. During those years I've written my family several times, and I've gotten letters back from two of my brothers but none from Ma or Pa. On the day before Christmas, 1829, I sit at the camp's big fire, feasting along with others on two elks brought in that day.

But in my mind I'm not eating with my fellow trappers. I'm at home in Ohio at the Christmas dinner I will miss tomorrow, at the table with Ma, Pa, my sisters, my brothers Ralph, Peter, Ira, and Austin, and Ralph's father-in-law, Dr. S. A. Simons. This is a room and a table I don't recognize—the family has moved from Pennsylvania since I was last at home.

I can't hear the conversation of my family word by word, but I can see their faces and feel the warmth in whatever they say, the support of each other, the togetherness. The love—I miss the love that binds everyone at that table into family. I hope they speak some words in memory of their brother Jedediah Strong Smith, resident of the faraway Rocky Mountains.

Though my middle name is Strong, my strength doesn't embrace being forgotten.

When I have filled my belly, I go to my own buffalo robe and blankets, gather tinder, strike sparks with my fire steel, and build a small fire for myself. Then I write a letter to my mother and father, beginning "Your unworthy Son once more undertakes to address his much slighted Parents."

Now I express my regret at not hearing from those parents since I left home and my desire to get fuller news of my family. I say

It is a long time since I left home & many times I have been ready to bring my business to a close & endeavor to come home—but have been hindered hitherto—as our business is at present it would be the height of impolicy to set a time to come Home. However, I will endeavor, by the assistance of Divine Providence, to come home as soon as possible. The greatest pleasure I could enjoy would be to accompany or be in company with my friends, but whether I shall ever be allowed the privilege, God only knows. I feel the need of the watch and care of a Christian Church. You may well suppose that our society is of the roughest kind—men of good morals seldom enter into a business of this kind. I hope you will remember me before a Throne of grace.

Next I write that a full account of the particulars of what's happening in the mountains had better wait for a face-to-face meeting, and I ask my parents to write me in care of William Sublette in St. Louis.

I conclude,

May God in his infinite mercy allow me soon to join my Parents is the prayer of your undutiful
Son, Jedediah S. Smith

Next I write a letter to my brother Ralph. Expressing regret that I have seldom gotten letters from my family members since coming to the mountains, I say I'm sure they wrote—the letters must have miscarried between Ohio and the Rockies, California, or wherever I've been.

Then I give a general account of what I have done since coming to the mountains, and my memories speak of the pain in my heart:

> I have passed through the country from St. Louis, Missouri, to the North Pacific Ocean, in different ways—through countries of barrenness and seldom the reverse. Many hostile tribes of Indians inhabit this space, and we are under the necessity of keeping a constant watch; notwithstanding our vigilance we sometime suffer; in August, 1827, ten men, who were in company with me, lost their lives by the Mojave Indians on the Colorado River; and in July,1828, fifteen men who were in company with me lost their lives by the Umpqua Indians, by the river of the same name... Many others lost their lives in different parts of the country—my brother believe me we have many dangers to face & many difficulties to encounter, but if I am spared I am not anxious with regard to difficulties—for particulars you must await a meeting—

I see that my little fire is down to coals, add some sticks to it, and fan it with my hat until it springs into a flame.

> As respects my Spiritual welfare, I hardly durst speak. I find myself one of the most ungrateful, unthankful creatures imaginable. Oh, when shall I be in the care of a Christian church? I have need of your prayers. I wish our Society to bear me up before a Throne of Grace—I cannot speak to my friends with regard to my coming home. I have set

so many times & have always found myself unable to perform that it is better to omit it. Give my love to my father, mother, brothers, sisters, nephews, & nieces, none excepted,
> I remain as ever your affectionate brother,
> Jedediah S. Smith

I write an addendum to Ralph on the back side of those same pages. Here I say that I'm giving a sum of two thousand dollars to him to distribute to family and friends. I add that the money is to be given anonymously. It is to go to our parents and to Dr. Simons. Some funds are to be used educating our brothers. Peter and Austin, though, need no help, since they are grown and embarked on trades. I promise to send more money, as needed, and ask Ralph's advice about who may need the money.

This letter eases a lot of my feelings of delinquency in my relationship with my family.

It also confesses that I walk inescapably with the spirits of twenty-five men who have died under my command.

Here at the end of my long addendum to brother Ralph I let forth—I admit it—a plea for understanding:

> It is that I may be able to help those who stand in need, that I face every danger—it is for this that I traverse the mountains covered with eternal snow—it is for this that I pass over the sandy plains in heat of summer, thirsting for water, and am well pleased if I can find a shade instead of water, where I may cool my overheated body—it is for this that I go for days without eating & am pretty well satisfied if I can gather a few roots, a few snails, or much better

satisfied if we can afford ourselves a piece of horseflesh or a fine roasted dog, and most of all it is for this that I deprive myself of the privilege of Society & the Satisfaction of the Converse of my friends. Oh my brother let us render to him to whom all things belong a proper proportion of what is his due. I must tell you that for my part I am much behind hand, oh! The perverseness of my wicked heart! I entangle myself all too much together in the things of time. I must depend entirely on the mercy of the being who is abundant in goodness and will not cast off any who call sincerely upon him. Again I say, pray for me my brother—and may he before whom not a sparrow falls without notice bring us in his own good time together again.

I set down my pencil and my journal and look long at the flickering flames. I reread what I have written to Ralph. I take several deep breaths in and out and admit it to myself. In this long letter, unexpectedly, I have put myself in a new situation: How long do I want to stay in this mountain life?

Chapter Twenty-One

After finishing that letter to my brother, I feel odd. I'm in a different frame of mind about everything. I get up and seek out Bill Sublette. My partner is packing up with Black Harris, who is known as a man of big leg—he can travel great distances on foot comfortably, for instance all the way to St. Louis in mid-winter, no problem.

I hold out my letters home to Sublette. My partner takes them with a reminder: "Two other men are waiting for you to write letters home for them."

I accept with a nod.

Harris says, "Them thar letters is sech as is gonna be packs of lies. Not one critter out here gonna tell his family the truth on how mountain life, it really be."

Sublette and I just grin.

"This hoss," Harris goes on, "now this hoss'll be glad and then around agin to make this trip to St. Louis. Now I says once more, this child is gonna cheat them plains out of his old bones."

More grins.

"That Saint Louy, though, this hoss ain't gonna stay in them doin's a day longer'n he hasta."

Sublette haw-haws. "You don't like the city of sin?" Bill teases his friend. "Why first thing in St. Louy you'll tyin' on a big one, and second you'll be bedding a riverfront whore."

I decide to let myself fall into the spirit of the kidding. "Then you'll go downstairs to the bar, find yourself a newspaperman, and tell him a few whoppers."

"You're the king of the whoppers," Bill puts in.

I add, "And those newspapers live on whoppers."

Then I leave them to their tomfoolery and their packing. I find Jim Bridger telling tall tales to Tom Fitzpatrick and Joe Meek at another fire. I squat on the balls of my feet and listen. I hear about the winter when the snow 'round the Salt Lake was fifty-foot deep and the buffler was froze so near the top only their heads was sticking out and one, *one-only shot* would bring a hungry man a feast. After I listen to this yarn again, I ask Old Jim about a section of Blackfoot country that I don't know. I intend to do one more big hunt before I quit on my partners.

Jim obliges me by pulling a buffalo hide over and sketching rivers, canyons, and ridges with the burnt end of a stick. He knows that country the way a farmer knows his back forty. When I have a good idea of where I want to go, I stand up and say to Bridger, "How about you come with me as a guide? I'll pay a bonus."

"Sho' nuff," says Bridger. "Count this child in."

Black Harris, who has been listening in the shadows, comes in and sits down by the fire. "Cap'n Smith, this child would follow you into the horrors of hell," he says. "But I know this. You ain't gonna follow me upstairs in no St. Louy whorehouse."

That gets a good laugh.

"Better whorehouses than schools and churches and stores," says Meek.

"We is Adams in the Garden of Eden," Bridger says, "goin' round and round without no rules, livin' off nature's bounty like *natural* men. Who *like* women."

I get up and start away from the fire, headed for my blankets. I find my friend Fitzpatrick walking beside me.

"Diah," he says, "I worry about you. You shame yourself about hanging about with the likes of Harris and Bridger."

I give Tom what must be a strange look.

"Your trouble is, you're after the Fall." Pause. "What's weighing on your shoulders is the consciousness of sin."

I stop, uncertain.

"Shrug those shoulders," says Tom.

⁂

The Wind River usually makes a good winter camp. This winter of 1829-30, though, is so cold that it drives the game to lower elevations. I follow with my brigade. We call a halt on the Powder River, a couple of hundred miles east. About April 1, I start the outfit toward Blackfoot country for that big, final hunt. Jim Bridger is my guide, and Joe Meek has joined the outfit.

As we trap the Musselshell and Judith Rivers, the Blackfeet hound us, daylight and darkness. During the day we gain in plews, but at night we lose it back in disappearing horses and traps.

When I give the order to get out of here, the men are glad to escape with a good crop of furs, still enough horses to ride, and our scalps. We circle back via the Big Horn and get into the rendezvous of 1830 on the Wind River with a good catch. I've done my part for Smith, Jackson, and Sublette.

Partner Davey Jackson is already there with plenty of beaver. When Bill Sublette comes in with the pack train and new outfit from St. Louis, our firm will be able to send our best take yet back downriver.

Unfortunately, in addition to enough supplies to carry the trappers through another year in the wilderness, Sublette comes with bad news. John Jacob Astor is headed to the mountains with his gigantic American Fur Company to compete with us. Astor is known to have huge amounts of capital and to be absolutely ruthless. Goliath is about to stomp on our little firm.

Change takes over fast. Davey, Bill, and I sell our business to a new bunch of partners, all good men—Tom Fitzpatrick, Jim Bridger, Milton Sublette, Henry Fraeb, and Jean Baptiste Gervais, who set up themselves up as the Rocky Mountain Fur Company. Their leadership is by mountain man, not businessman. Old Gabe Bridger is a legend among trappers, though illiterate. Fraeb and Gervais are experienced booshways. Milton Sublette knows the mountains. Tom Fitzpatrick will be the brains of the outfit.

No one knows whether this daring new partnership can withstand the onslaught of Astor and his American Fur Company. I think my friend Fitz may be smart enough to pull it off. Astor's people will be beginners here in the mountains, and are bound to trip over their own feet.

I'm relieved that we've sold our business—I'm freed of a big connection to the mountains and my partners.

The firm of Smith, Jackson, and Sublette has come out of this deal smelling like roses. After all our ups and downs, we are going home with a profit of $54,000. In St. Louis we can take up the roles of wealthy businessmen.

The newspapers will salute us as heralds of the westward expansion of the American people.

When I publish them, my maps will contribute to that expansion.

Yes, our trapper comrades left in the mountains will laugh at the idea of so-called civilization coming their way. And maybe, underneath, they'll be scared by the thought of the land they love getting rutted by wagon wheels, swept with brooms, and frilled with skirts.

But they can't make the tide go out when it's coming in. As 1830 rolls along, the opportunities of the wide, wide West will come to the attention of a large majority of Americans for the first time—and people will be stirred.

ख़

In St. Louis I have personal business to get settled. I send brother Ralph some money to buy a farm back in Ohio. *Maybe*, I'm thinking, *I'll become a farmer*. Meanwhile, I need a place to live in St. Louis.

My brothers Peter, Austin, and Ira show up. I write home to say that St. Louis is no place to send youngsters—it reeks with temptations. To accommodate the family I already have in St. Louis, I buy a house and lot on Federal Avenue and add two black slaves as household staff, a situation suitable for a prosperous man of affairs.

I get unhappy news from home. My mother has died. That makes me feel even more urgency about taking care of my three brothers in St. Louis. At least I've given them a place to live.

Now I want to make progress on getting my journals and maps ready for publication. I hire a young man named

Jedediah Smith

Samuel Parkman to copy the journals and aid in drafting my maps. I look forward to establishing a reputation as an author and an explorer.

Next—what should I do with the capital I've accumulated? My share of the Smith, Jackson, and Sublette's earnings is big. In the tradition of my church this is an important accomplishment. Making money is a virtue, and letting capital go unused would be a sin. So I need to put my capital somewhere it will grow.

Brother Peter wants to make a success like mine in the mountains. Brother Austin is casting about for something to do. Brother Ira is also at loose ends.

So I start thinking about being a trader again.

I won't go back to the life of a humble hunter of the beaver, as I described myself to the governor of California. No, I will be more like General Ashley, who started as a businessman of the fur trade, made a fortune, and now is a member of the U.S. House of Representatives for Missouri.

And so I allow myself to toy with the idea of going west as a trader, perhaps to Santa Fe, where a good route and substantial trade have been established. Perhaps even to the Mexican provinces beyond.

The Santa Fe Trail does not go through the mountains, or near beaver country. It winds across the plains past Indian tribes accustomed to white traders and mostly peaceable.

Yes, I can see myself in a new way, as a man who lives in a fine house in St. Louis and trades to Santa Fe. I will publish my journals as a book and will help my country by publishing my maps and correcting the mistaken ideas about the West.

That settles it. I will become a trader. The Santa Fe Trail has been pioneered by William Becknell a decade ago and is well established. It goes through a country thick with buffalo. True, the Comanches can be contrary, but the traders who use the trail say that even those Indians will eventually become good trading partners.

My mind is made up. I've returned to civilization and find that I need a challenge. This is not just the trail calling to me, or giving in to my wayfaring heart. This is good sense. It's giving my brothers Peter and Austin a start in the world.

Santa Fe will be a grand adventure.

Chapter Twenty-Two

Plans are also changing for my former partners. Jackson and Sublette have been expecting word from Tom Fitzpatrick confirming that they should bring supplies to the rendezvous of 1831—that's their deal.

But Fitz hasn't shown up.

Bill and Davey have already bought supplies for the rendezvous. But no word confirming that Fitz and partners want supplies. What to do?

We talk and decide that Bill and Davey will ride to Santa Fe with me and trade their goods there. We'll keep the two businesses separate, theirs and mine, each operating under its own license and making its own sales, but we'll unite into one big train of horses and mules for the trip. There's safety in numbers. After Santa Fe I'm free to go wherever I want to go.

We start out from St. Louis on April 10 with an impressive train—seventy-four men, twenty-two wagons, and a six-pound cannon. We march west across Missouri to Lexington and cut spare axles for the rolling plains ahead. Those plains will be nearly treeless. But we look forward to two hundred miles of grasses before any likely troubles with the unpredictable Comanches.

Meanwhile, in this camp we get a delightful surprise. Tom Fitzpatrick rides in.

We three partners jump up from our evening fire. We pound Fitz on the back.

"Great to see you, Pard!"

"Have some coffee, friend."

And in mock imitation of mountain style, "Glad you be above ground, Fitz!"

I brace Tom by both shoulders. He's as good a friend as they get.

He sits down, coffee cup in hand, and says, "Okay, what you want to know is, do we want to be supplied for rendezvous? Our answer is, damn right! Sure we do! We got a couple of hundred men to re-supply and a big bunch of Indians to trade with."

Uh-oh. Bill and Davey are intending to sell their goods in Santa Fe.

Then Fitz explains why he's late: Four of the partners of the new Rocky Mountain Fur Company went back to Blackfoot country, including him. The other two went to Shoshone country. The four got no word from the two about sending the express to St. Louis.

"After too damn long," Fitz goes on, "my partners decided to go ahead and have this crazy Irishman take the express."

The problem is that "too damn long" means the express is two months late. The message that was due in March has arrived in May, and now the rendezvous to be supplied starts in two short months.

Davey, Bill, and I want to help our friend, but we're on a different mission. So we go into council, chew it back and forth a bit, and come out with a proposal.

I say, "Tom, if you'll ride to Santa Fe with us, we'll supply you there."

151

Davey adds, "Me and Bill will get together two-thirds of your outfit, Diah the other third."

The problem is that we'll be giving the supplies to Fitz in mid-June, and he'll be at least a month late getting to rendezvous. Lots of trappers and Indians will be waiting impatiently.

Fitz shrugs. "It's me who got the late start."

༄

Near Council Grove our train gets a surprise attack by Indians that even we mountain men can't identify. All we care about, though, is that the cannon drives them off. But the four of us have the same thought: Maybe the Santa Fe Trail isn't as trouble-free as we've heard.

Fitz delights everyone by bringing new life to our camp fires.

The train has already been enjoying some entertainment in the evenings. Davey hired an Irishman by the name of Paddy O'Shea as his clerk. When he took O'Shea on, the Irishman signed his name just "Paddy."

"Is Paddy the only name you got?" inquired Davey.

"No," said the applicant, "it ain't. My name is Michael O'Shea. But since I'm Irish, I know the lads will call me Paddy anyway, and I give in to it."

Davey listed Paddy as hired.

The pleasure of having Paddy along is that he adds a lot of fun to our nightly fires. He plays the fiddle in what he says is the Donegal style. Whatever the style, everyone gets a kick out of his lively tunes, which set us to tapping our feet and clapping our hands.

When he finds a willing dancer, Paddy teaches the fellow some steps of the jig. According to Paddy, the trick is to catch on to a step called the rise and grind. Paddy demonstrates over and over— "Hop, hop back—hop, hop back" he calls. But there's a problem. When Paddy is busy demonstrating and his fiddle isn't singing out, only he can catch on to how the steps coordinate with the music.

Big change: Now Tom Fitzpatrick, an Irishman through and through, has joined our train, so we have an Irish fiddler and an Irish dancer.

They decline to entertain each evening until the meat has gotten done just right and their bellies are filled with warmth.

Sometimes one of the other hands gets up and tries the hop, hop back. Each one, though, gets his feet tangled and ends up in the dust. Paddy accompanies each collapse with a dramatic series of descending notes and an ominous double stop.

One night Fitz gets a little drunk and comes after me— "Get out here and try it. Hop, hop back, hop, hop back, there's nothing to it."

I grin and wave the idea off.

Then a couple of men begin to clap and chant, "Captain Smith! Capitano Smith!"

Soon all are clapping and chanting.

I struggle to my feet, call out, "No promises!" and stand ready.

Paddy launches into a jig. Fitz jumps in front of me and starts modelling the steps. Then he adds a call—"Hop, hop back, hop, hop back."

I start tentatively but then put some energy into it. Here comes more energy, and I join in calling out, "Hop, hop back, hop, hop back." On my fourth cry of "hop back," I plop down hard on my butt.

A burst of laughter and applause.

Fitz helps me up with both hands, then supports me with a hand around my back, and says to the circle, "Guess what?" He points to my chest. "There's a live one in here somewhere, ain't there?"

Lots more laughter.

Though his steps are unsteady from drink, Tom takes me by an elbow and leads me back from the fire. "Let's sit here," he says. "We'll be at what fancy folks call the penumbra of the firelight."

I smile, and we sit down cross-legged. Tom has more words in his head than any other mountain man.

He says, "I've gotta ask you this. You said you wanted to be in St. Louis to be in the embrace of a Christian church, yet you no more'n get there than you're on the trail again. It's about time you wake up to something."

"What's that?" I ask, tickled.

"Listen to that wily heart of yours. It's telling you you're in love with the wi-i-lds." He makes that last word sing.

Now Tom takes thought, twists his mouth in a funny way, and goes on, slurring his words a little. "Now this here child knows his loyalties. Atalanta, the Greek goddess of adventure; Abeona, the Roman Goddess of Outward Journeys, and Adiona, the Goddess of Safe Return; Ekehau, Mayan God of travelers and merchants. I ride flying those flags."

Tom puts his hand on his heart.

"The *New Testament*? That one don't fly, not in this country."

He drops the hand.

⁕

As our train moves up the Arkansas River, we endure the long-lasting drizzles, mires, the irritable behavior of the mules, and trouble getting our twenty-two wagons across the swollen creeks.

Then nature turns over and lies on her other side. We come to the Cimarron Cutoff, a shortcut from the Arkansas River to the Cimarron River. The Cimarron is what I call an Inconstant River, one of those streams that gives a water hole here, then a long stretch of flowing underground, and a water hole there, followed by far too much distance underground.

We could go along the Arkansas to the Rockies, turn left, and go through Raton Pass to Santa Fe. But that route is longer and we're behind time already, especially with Fitz getting later and later to rendezvous.

We take the Cutoff. It's a water scrape, forty or fifty waterless miles to a river that plays hide and seek. I give it thought first. I've gone ahead fifty times to find water, and I have a knack for it.

In the first three days we come to no water at all. And the land is cut up by countless buffalo trails, which confuse the route. Our horses and mules are dying from thirst. The men are half-delirious.

It's time for me to step up.

Taking Fitz along, I push ahead looking for a water hole or a spring.

Jedediah Smith

Nothing.
More nothing.
Somewhere ahead is the Cimarron River, but...
We come to a hole that should have water, but it's dry.
"Fitz," I say, "dig here. Get water. And when the train gets here and has a drink, point out the direction I've gone."
I can see reluctance in Tom's face.
I say, "This is what I do."
I ride ahead, alone in Indian country. That's risky, but someone has to take a chance and find water. "Someone" usually points to me. Which is OK.
I ride about fifteen miles further south and come to the dry bed of the Cimarron.
I find one of the holes the buffalo probably use.
Pause for caution.
No, I need water, and my horse needs water.
I ease the reins, let my mount walk in, and step in thigh-deep.
Cool liquid. Salvation for the whole train when they get here. I dunk my face and swallow.
When I look up, I see that I'm half-circled by Comanches, fifteen or twenty of them.
My chances are slim.
My one hope is to make a strong front of it. I swing onto my horse, ride straight toward the chief, and make the signs for peace.
The Comanches pay no attention. They fan out.
I make peace signs to the chief again.
No response.
My mount edges back.
Suddenly the Comanches shout at my horse and wave their blankets at us.

My mount wheels, turning my flank to some of the Indians.

I hear the sound of a shot and feel like my left shoulder has been sledge-hammered. My breath is ripped away.

I rein my horse to the front, level my Hawken, and kill the chief.

I grab for my pistols. A lance knocks my arm away from a handle. Two more shots are simultaneous with two more sledge-hammer blows, these to my chest.

As I lose my balance, lances assault me. I fall back and sideways, an unreal sensation like a dream. I hit the ground hard.

The sky blinks out.

It doesn't come back.

Fitz

Soon my digging pays off and the hole is filling with water. Lots of water. I lead my horse in and we wallow in it.

Then I lead the horse out of the water and scout the horizon to the north. There's the outfit, scattered out looking for me and Diah. As they come to the hole, I realize that every nerve in my body is saying, Diah's in trouble.

After everyone drinks, we try to follow Diah's trail across the arid land. But the numberless buffalo trails that crisscross his route obliterate his sign.

We don't find his body.

Eventually, the outfit moves on and keep moving to find real water, the actual Cimarron River, not just liquid that's here and there.

Peter and Austin, Diah's brothers, stay behind, and I stay with them. We three search up and down the sequence of holes spotted to the left and right, to no avail. At last, in the fading light, we follow the wide trail of the train's many animals to the caravan's camp by the actual Cimarron River.

༄

When we get to Santa Fe on July 4, we hear the story of Diah's death from some Mexican traders who have his rifle and pistols. They got the weapons, and the story, from the Comanches.

Peter and Austin buy their brother's weapons from the traders.

I compose a eulogy for him in my journal, my tribute to a remarkable man and a great friend:

> Jedediah, your body lies alone in a wasteland, observed only by the sun that circles above you every day and the moon that lights you by night. Mother Earth knows you made altars of her mountaintops. She remembers that you sipped the sweetness of her mountain creeks as the grace of God. She knows you made an understanding of her myriad ways into your sacraments. You treasured her so much you took numberless steps on her surface, and saw more of her bounty than any other man of your time. She knows you loved her.
>
> Now she welcomes you home.

THE END

Printed in Dunstable, United Kingdom